GRANDFATHER'S CHRISTMAS ORPHANS

Victorian Romance

FAYE GODWIN

Tica House
Publishing

Sweet Romance that Delights and Enchants!

Copyright © 2023 by Faye Godwin

All rights reserved.

No part of this book may be reproduced in any form or by any electronic or mechanical means, including information storage and retrieval systems, without written permission from the author, except for the use of brief quotations in a book review.

PERSONAL WORD FROM THE AUTHOR

DEAREST READERS,

I'm so delighted that you have chosen one of my books to read. I am proud to be a part of the team of writers at Tica House Publishing. Our goal is to inspire, entertain, and give you many hours of reading pleasure. Your kind words and loving readership are deeply appreciated.

I would like to personally invite you to sign up for updates and to become part of our **Exclusive Reader Club**—it's completely Free to Join! I'd love to welcome you!

Much love,

Faye Godwin

FAYE GODWIN

CLICK HERE to Join our Reader's Club and to Receive Tica House Updates!

https://victorian.subscribemenow.com/

CONTENTS

Personal Word From The Author — 1

PART I
Chapter 1 — 7
Chapter 2 — 21
Chapter 3 — 34
Chapter 4 — 47
Chapter 5 — 58
Chapter 6 — 76

PART II
Chapter 7 — 89
Chapter 8 — 105
Chapter 9 — 118
Chapter 10 — 130

PART III
Chapter 11 — 139
Chapter 12 — 162
Chapter 13 — 176

PART IV
Chapter 14 — 187
Chapter 15 — 198

Epilogue — 212
Chapter 1 — 213
Continue Reading... — 219
Thanks For Reading — 222

More Faye Godwin Victorian Romances! — 223
About the Author — 225

CHAPTER 1

The cottage smelled like the sea, even though the windows were all closed, and the curtains were drawn against the biting wind that wailed mournfully through the eaves of the cottage. The sound disguised the soft padding of Alice's shoes on the warm carpet as she tiptoed through the dining room, a hand clasped over her mouth to keep her giggles from escaping.

The thing about finding her smallest sister, Hester, was that there were only three places she ever hid in this room: behind the drapes, underneath the sideboard, or squeezed tightly into the gap between the dusty old clarinet under its cover and the wall. Grandfather always shouted if he saw fingerprints on the cover, but it *was* an excellent hiding place, Alice had to admit to herself. Or at least it had been, the first sixty or seventy times.

Now she didn't even bother looking anywhere else. Alice's eyes darted to the clarinet, the sideboard, and the drapes, and she knew that if she stood still enough for just a few seconds longer, in total silence, the suspense would overwhelm five-year-old Hester.

Alice bit her lip to hold back her giggles. A second later, her silence paid off. The drapes twitched. Still in total silence, Alice slunk across the floor like a stalking fox. She reached out a hand, heart thudding, and approached the drapes ever so slowly.

Hester's nerve failed her when Alice was just six feet away. She burst out from behind the drapes with a drawn-out squeal of laughter, and Alice raced after her, giggling.

"Come here, you," she yelled.

Hester shrieked gleefully and fell on her hands and knees to crawl under the dining table, her little body fitting easily between the chair legs.

"Hey," Alice laughed. "No fair."

Hester popped out from between the chair legs and bolted for the open door. Alice raced after her, and the little girl was quick, but Alice had five years and several inches of leg on her. She dived and her fingertips brushed the back of Hester's faded dress.

"Got you," Alice giggled.

Hester slowed enough that Alice could grab the little girl in her arms and tickle her. Hester's peals of laughter rang through the house, drowning out the mournful wail of the wind. Alice was grateful for them. The wind always sounded so lonely and sad when it blew like that.

The broom cupboard door opened, and another little girl tumbled out, only slightly older than Hester. Her blonde hair was neatly plaited and tied up under her bonnet. "I win." she announced.

"No you don't, Betty." Hester jerked herself out of Alice's arms. "Allie hadn't started looking for you yet."

"She found *you*," Betty retorted, "and she caught you, so I win."

"If she'd caught *you*, she'd have won," Hester complained.

"All right, all right," Alice laughed. "There's no point arguing."

Hester gave Betty a simmering look from underneath the mop of unruly brown hair that never seemed certain if it was curly or just a mess.

Alice knew that this could rapidly become a bloodbath. "Who's ready for lunch?" she said.

The girls instantly brightened and scampered over to the little kitchen. The dining room was the cottage's only extravagance; the kitchen was so small that Grandfather and the three girls barely fit inside, but it was Alice's favorite place in

ALICE'S FEET crunched on slush. Early this morning, when Grandfather kissed the girls goodbye, their street had been covered in soft white snow. Even the beach was sparkly white under the pale morning light. Now, feet and smog and wheels and hooves had churned that shiny whiteness into a mush of yellow-grey, peppered with road apples and cigarette butts.

"Hester," Alice yelled. "Not so far."

The little girl had been running down the path ahead of her and stumbled to a halt. Her breath curled as steam around her face, cheeks red with the cold, eyes shining. "Grandpapa," she squealed.

"We'll see him in a minute," said Alice.

Betty trudged along beside Alice, her arms wrapped around her body in her fat, fluffy coat. She seldom ran ahead the way Hester did, but her keen grey eyes flashed around, taking in everything: the donkey cart that plodded past; the boys throwing stones into the sea from the beach; the thin, stooped old man who traipsed along the water's edge along the freezing sand, bending to pick up bits of glass left behind by the tide.

Alice tried not to look at any of this as they caught up to Hester. It was only twenty minutes' walk to Grandfather's northern fish stand—the one in the south was deeper inside the city, or at least, so he said; he would never let the girls go there—and that meant that the girls only had about an hour outside the cottage every day. Alice was determined to make the most of it. She trained her eyes on the blurry grey horizon, watching the whitecaps form as the waves rolled slowly in. There was a ship on the horizon, she thought. She could see the stern black line of its mast against the sky. It must be waiting to come to the docks.

They reached the top of the last little hill and looked down at the sprawl of London. It vanished into a smoggy horizon, but what Alice could see was a black smear on the seaside, a seething mass of little squat buildings with winding alleyways that swarmed with people. The docks stretched as far as Alice could see, ship after ship resting against the wooden piers, stacked with boxes, nets, and barrels. People swarmed over the ships, scrambled along the docks, and strode in a tight-packed mass along the street that wandered against the docks.

"I'm glad we don't have to go all the way down there with all those people," said Betty.

"People are fun," Hester squealed.

Alice laughed. "They *are* fun."

Their route took them along a desolate little footpath with littered edges, frequented by few. A vast trading ship, its gangplanks drawn up, rocked on the grey water up ahead, blocking their view of the fish stand. The path under their feet turned from mud to stone, and then a creature burst out from behind a pile of broken old barrels. She was so stooped and hunchbacked that she barely looked human, with yellowed claws for hands and wild, white-rimmed eyes surrounded by a stringy cloud of hair the brownish-grey of the smog.

Hester screamed blue murder. She fled behind Alice, clinging to her skirts, as the old hag hobbled nearer.

"Pretty little girls," she hissed. "Pretty little precious girls."

Betty clutched Alice's hand, and Alice pulled her close. She kept walking, making a wide arc around the hag.

The old woman didn't stop. She limped after them with surprising speed. "Such pretty girls. Fetch a pretty price. Don't you want to come with me? Sweetmeats and toys. Come along with me."

"Sweetmeats?" Hester slowed.

"Don't you dare, Hester," Alice snapped.

The woman caught up to them, and her old, clawed hand shot out and grazed Alice's arm. "Pretty—"

"Go away." Alice whirled around.

The woman withdrew with a catlike hiss but hovered a few feet away.

Alice strode forward, arms folded. "I told you to go away. Leave my sisters and I alone."

Hester and Betty whimpered with fear.

The old woman curled a lip, revealing black and toothless gums, but Alice raised her chin. "I mean it."

The hag's eyes narrowed. She turned and limped off, muttering, and shaking her head in uncoordinated little twitches, and Alice exhaled slowly.

"Come on, you two." She grabbed her sisters' hands.

The sound of running feet made her jump, but Hester squealed, "Charlie." and pulled free. Alice relaxed and watched the little girl run up to the boy who jogged up the hill to meet them. He wore a cloth cap and a tattered red neckerchief, and his eyes were round and worried in a dirty, tar-streaked face.

"Are you all right?" he called.

Hester hugged him around the knees. "We're all right, Charlie."

"We're fine," said Alice. "That old lady was just a bit scary, but harmless."

"I don't know." Charlie frowned, his sunny blue eyes worried. "I'll walk the rest of the way with you, if you like."

Alice couldn't help smiling. "I *do* like, but don't tell Grandfather, all right?"

"No." Hester shook her head rapidly. "We don't tell Grandpapa about anything that happens on walks."

"Or we won't get to go on walks at all," Betty chipped in. "Allie had to beg and beg and beg for him to let us come to see him at all."

"All right," Charlie laughed. "Just be careful, all right?"

He squinted at them with the worldly concern of someone who was eleven, worked at the docks and had seen the evils of this place. Alice thought that it gave him a splendidly grown-up air. She giggled a little as he took Hester's hand, and they fell into step toward the fish stand together while he told them about the big, beautiful ship that had come into the docks that morning all the way from India.

"Spices, Allie. Smells you'd never even dreamed of," he said. "And silk. Big bolts of it. I've never seen anything so shiny."

"Wow," Hester whispered, round-eyed.

"Did you see any tigers?" Alice asked as they rounded the big ship and the fish stand came into view. "Grandpapa says he's heard that there are tigers in India."

"What's a tiger?" asked Hester.

"Like a very big cat," said Charlie. "A mean one."

Betty shivered. "I don't think I want to meet a tiger."

"You won't," said Charlie. "The ship didn't bring any. I asked."

The fish stand perched at the edge of the docks, right next to the little boat that Grandfather said he used to fish on

"You two run along ahead," Grandfather ordered. "I need to talk to Allie for a minute."

Betty stomped off, pouting, while Hester scampered eagerly several yards in front.

Even though she was ten, Alice allowed herself the momentary indignity of slipping her small hand inside her grandfather's big, rough one. His stubby fingers closed over hers.

"What's the matter, Grandpapa?" she asked softly. "Did I do something wrong?"

"No, poppet." Grandfather studied her for a few moments, his eyes gentle. "Did anyone ever tell you how much you look like your mother?"

Alice blushed. "Sometimes."

"Well, you do. You look just like her," Grandfather told her. "The same hair." He playfully tweaked one of the chaotic black corkscrews that sprouted from underneath Alice's bonnet.

She giggled.

"I worry for all of you," said Grandfather softly. "Won't you stay in the cottage until I get back from the stand? We could go for walks afterwards."

Alice gazed across the docks. Darkness had almost completely fallen now; the golden haloes of lanterns shed most of the light. "There wouldn't be time. It'd be dark, Grandpapa, and you'd be so tired."

He sighed. "It's not safe, you know."

"I'll keep us safe," Alice promised. "I will. But we can't stay inside all the time, Grandpapa. We're so, so bored. Every day, we can't wait to come and see you."

Grandfather held up a hand. "And I won't make you. But I beg you, my poppet, be careful." He wrapped his arm around her shoulders and pulled her close to his rough, scratchy coat. "The world is full of horrors for little girls like you."

Alice leaned against him. "Not when they have grandpapas like you."

He laughed, a rolling barrel of sound.

CHAPTER 2

DESPITE HER ASSERTIONS, Alice heard Grandfather's words over and over in her head the next day as they set off to get him. She kept a sharp eye on Hester as she scampered along the road in front of her. Gloaming settled across the seaside, thick as the smog, and the first few lanterns had already been lit before they'd even set out. It must be nearly Christmas, Alice thought, if the nights had already grown so long.

The world is full of horrors for little girls like you. Alice wondered what Grandfather meant. She hoped she'd never have to find out.

The heap of broken barrels loomed ahead, like a crouching beast, and Alice stopped. "Hester." she shouted. "Get back here."

Hester kept running, giggling and heedless.

Her hands had almost stopped shaking when they reached Grandfather's fish stand, but only almost.

Saturday afternoons, Alice had decided, were the best times of the entire week.

She sat on the crumbling old wooden bench in the corner of the strip of garden behind the cottage, enjoying the rare, balmy sunshine that poured out of the pale blue sky. Grandfather always said that sunshine in December came right before a blizzard. Maybe he was right, but for now, Alice was going to enjoy it.

A few feet away, Hester and Betty sat side by side against the tall brick wall of the garden, enjoying the slices of rabbit pie that Alice had cut for them. She'd finished hers, which wasn't surprising; she'd cut herself only a sliver. The lion's share had gone to Charlie.

He was polishing the last of it off in big, hungry gulps now, and Alice smiled as she watched. He never said it, but she knew that most of the food in their house went to his baby sisters. He and his mother both worked at the docks, and Grandfather had said that that was a hard life for anyone, let alone a woman and a child.

At least it meant that on Saturday afternoons, his mother stayed home with the baby and Charlie could do whatever he wanted. To Alice's astonishment, that turned out to be playing with Alice and her sisters.

"Thanks, Allie." Charlie handed her his plate. "That was really good."

"I'm glad you liked it," said Alice. She took their plates and piled them on the bench beside her; she'd wash them later, when Charlie had to go home. For now, she wanted to spend all the time she could with him.

"Say," said Charlie, "why don't we go down to the beach and play with the other children there? It'd be fun."

"Shhh," said Alice. "Not so loud in front of the little ones. I don't want them to be upset."

"Upset? Why?"

"Because we can't play on the beach with the others," Alice sighed. "The other children don't like us."

Charlie frowned. "Whyever not?"

"They say we're lazy. Their mamas have told them not to play with us in case they get lazy, like us."

"I see," said Charlie. "It's because you don't go to work." He tilted his head to one side. "Why don't you?"

"Grandfather says it's not right for children to work. He says that we should be playing and learning to grow up," said Alice, "or at school. He's always sad because he can't send us to school."

"At least you don't have to work," said Charlie, "which must be wonderful."

"It *is* wonderful," Alice agreed, "but it would be more wonderful if you could play with us more often."

Charlie laughed. "I think so, too." He swung his legs, enjoying the sun, and leaned back against the bench. "Maybe you'll grow up to be something fancy. Like a governess, or something."

Alice blushed. "I would like that very much."

"I'll be a sailor," Charlie decided. "Or, no—I'll be a shipwright."

"I like that idea," said Alice.

"But we'll always stay here by the sea," said Charlie. "Won't we?"

Alice met his eyes and smiled. "We will," she said, and meant it.

He met her eyes and grinned, then blushed and looked away. Alice wasn't sure what to do with the uncomfortable silence, so she said, "Do you know where we can find some mistletoe?"

"I'm sure," said Charlie. "There's some growing in a park near the docks. I walk by there when I walk my mama to work every morning."

"Oh, will you bring us some, please?" Alice begged. "Grandfather always says he's too busy for decorations, but I know he wants them. We could make the place look so pretty."

"All right. I'll bring you some."

"Thank you, Charlie." Alice hugged him tightly.

He hugged her back, and for a long moment, Alice didn't want to let go.

THE THICK GREEN fronds of mistletoe hung everywhere in the cottage. Alice didn't know how Charlie had succeeded in bringing so much home—he'd had to use both arms to carry the pile yesterday—but he had, and now the cottage looked more Christmassy than it ever had. The girls had made paper chains from old newspapers, too, and even cut out some bunting shapes as well. Now they hung in strings all over the kitchen, crisscrossing the roof, and they'd even draped a generous rope of mistletoe across the front door.

"Grandpapa is going to love it," Hester whispered.

"You're right, Hestie," Alice grinned. "He sure is. Let's go and get him."

The little girls clung to one another as Alice squared her shoulders and walked around to the back of the fish stand. Sure enough, Dorcas sat on the edge of the docks, her feet dangling above the murky brown-grey water. A net sprawled around her like the train of a wedding dress, and she worked on a section in her lap, her gnarled hands moving quickly.

Alice took a deep breath. "Dorcas? I mean—Miss Benson?"

Dorcas raised her head and glared. Her face was a lumpish, wrinkly mass dominated by a gigantic, hooked nose with warts on it.

"You should be working, child," she hissed. "Look at these hands." She held up her old hands, the joints swollen and twisted with work. "Let your young fingers do the work. But oh, no, old man Pryor's little granddaughters are far too precious for that." She spat into the sea; Alice heard the splash.

Alice swallowed. "Miss Benson, where's my grandfather?"

"How should I know?" Dorcas growled.

"I thought you might have seen him," said Alice, "or maybe you'll know if he left the stand this afternoon." She thought of the mistletoe and clutched her skirts with trembling fingers.

"'I thought you might have seen him'," Dorcas mocked. "Of course, I saw him. Ain't seeing him now, though."

"Well, yes," said Alice.

"Don't give me cheek, child," Dorcas sneered.

"I'm not," said Alice hurriedly. "I promise I'm not. I'm just wondering when last you saw him? Do you know where he went?"

"How'm I supposed to know?" snapped Dorcas. "I ain't seen him since noon."

Noon. Alice's heart thudded as she returned to the other girls after thanking Dorcas. That had been hours and hours ago. Had Grandfather been on his way back home to the cottage?

No, that didn't make sense. They would have met him along the road. He had to be in the city, at the second fish stand, the one that Alice had never seen, in the place where he would never let her go.

"Allie, what did she say?" Hester clutched at her skirt. "Where is he?"

All Alice's clever answers and assurances shrivelled up in the face of Hester's big, scared eyes. "I don't know."

"How can you not know?" Betty wailed. "Where is he?"

"I don't know, all right?" Alice snapped. She grabbed the girls' hands. "We'd better go looking for him."

"Where?" said Betty, wide-eyed.

"In the city, of course. Where his other fish stand is."

"The city," Hester quavered. She stared at the tight mass of buildings further south along the docks, the lanterns already lit, wisps of smoke rising from chimneys to join the black cloud of smog that blotted out the stars.

"No." Betty backed away, shaking her head. "No, we're not allowed to go there. Grandfather said—"

"Grandfather's not here, Betty," said Alice. "We must find him. What if he's in trouble? What if he's sick?"

Hester's lower lip trembled. "Sick?" she echoed.

Alice felt a pang of guilt. "I didn't mean it like that, Hestie."

"Then let's go back," said Betty urgently. "Right now. He'll come home. We can just wait for him there."

Alice squared her shoulders. "I'm going to look for him, whether you like it or not."

"Me too," said Hester.

Betty glared. "Then take me home first."

"There's no time for that." Alice couldn't stop thinking about the policeman that had come to their house, about the words he'd said to Grandfather. *There's been an accident.* She couldn't hear words like that ever again. Where would they go this time, if there was no more Grandfather to be with them?

"I can't go alone," Betty wailed.

Alice turned away, terror making her hands tremble. "I don't care, Betty. I'm going to find Grandfather. You can come or you can go home on your own."

She tugged at Hester's arm, and they set off together, heading into the jungle of darkness and buildings, the tangle of alleyways and smog ahead. It was several minutes before the sound of Betty's running footsteps caught up with them. Betty was sobbing, but Alice didn't look back.

Nothing else mattered, except for finding Grandfather.

"Ribbons." a thin girl whispered from the street corner. She was no older than Alice, and her flesh clung to her skeleton as if for warmth, her voice emanating hoarsely with illness. "Ribbons for your Christmas tree?"

She held up a handful of wrinkled, faded ribbons that hardly looked fit to tie up loose papers, never mind adorning anything.

They reached the end of the square, but every shop was closed and shuttered except for the loud place with the vomiting man. No streets led out of it; the only way out was the way they'd come.

"Where are we, Alice?" Hester whispered.

Betty's defiance had left her. Her face was grey and streaked with tears. "Are we lost?"

Alice clutched her hand tightly. "We're not lost."

"Then take us home," Betty begged.

Alice turned left and right, trying to get her bearings. If she followed the docks, she could get them home. But how to get back to the docks? And where was Grandfather? They still hadn't found him.

"I'm scared," Hester sobbed.

Alice scooped her up onto her hip and took Betty's hand. "Don't be scared. We'll be all right." But she looked back in the direction of the vomiting man and terror boiled in her belly.

The man was now leaning against the wall of the loud place, his beard still glittering with filth. Alice stuck to the far side of the square from him, holding Betty close and praying with all of her might that they'd get past him safely, that they'd find their way home, that Grandfather would be there waiting, cross and worried underneath the strings of mistletoe.

They were across the square from the man when he pushed off the wall and suddenly lurched forward, wagging a finger in their general direction. "Little lost Christmas angels, are you?" he slurred.

"Ignore him," Alice whispered. "Just ignore him."

"I'm scared," Betty wailed.

Hester clutched Alice's dress and sobbed.

"Lost angels," said the man, stumbling after them. "Oi. Oi. Look at them little lost things." He chortled.

Alice didn't know what he wanted with them, but goosebumps scattered on her body as he continued to follow them. Her heart fluttered, and tears stung her eyes.

No. Furious, Alice swallowed the lump in her throat. She wasn't going to cry, not in front of her sisters. She had to get Hester and Betty home and she had to find Grandfather, and if she was going to do that, she needed to pull herself together.

"Bet you smell nice," the man whispered. "Bet you smell nice, pretty little lost things." He stumbled nearer, and his hand brushed Alice's back.

Her fear condensed into white-hot anger. She whipped around. "Leave us alone."

But this man was not so easily cowed. His eyes narrowed, and he drew back a hand, curling it into a fist. "Think you can talk to me that way, little girl?"

Betty screamed, a high-pitched, whistling sound, let go of Alice's skirt and bolted.

"Betty!" Alice yelled. "Get back here."

She turned and chased after the child, Hester bouncing and sobbing on her hip. The man's laughter was the only thing that pursued them. Alice caught up to Betty halfway down the next block and grabbed her by the arm to yank her back.

"Stop. Stop," she ordered. "He's not chasing us. You're running away from something that isn't even there. Stop it."

Betty sobbed. "I'm so scared. Take me home, Alice."

"I'm trying," Alice shouted.

Betty shrank back, wide-eyed, and Alice forced herself to take a deep breath. "I'm trying," she said more gently.

She straightened up and gazed around the street, searching for anything that seemed familiar. Mistletoe was wrapped around the streetlights; in one window, she spotted a Christmas tree, all done up with bows and bright oranges. Only a handful of people moved on this street, and none of them paid the girls any mind. Most of them were old, shabby, homeless folk, but Alice's eyes caught suddenly on a youthful figure that strode along the street with a jaunty step.

Her heart thudded with hope. "Charlie?" she cried.

"It's him," said Hester.

"Charlie," Alice shouted.

Charlie stopped and looked around, frowning. When he spotted Alice and her sisters, his eyes grew huge.

"Alice," he called, jogging over the street to them. "Betty. Hester. What in heaven's name are you doing in a place like this at this time of night?"

"Oh, Charlie." Alice couldn't stop herself from throwing an arm around him. "We went to fetch Grandpapa, and he wasn't there. Dorcas said he was at the fish stand here in the city, so we came to find him, but we couldn't."

Betty and Hester sobbed, clinging to Charlie.

"Where are we?" Betty wailed. "Where's Grandpapa?"

"I don't know where he is," said Charlie. "He wasn't at the fish stand when I passed it just now."

She closed her eyes, tears rolling freely, and prayed. *Oh, please, please let my grandpapa be safe. Please bring him back to me.*

"It's going to be all right, Allie," said Charlie.

"I hope so," said Alice. She opened her eyes and swallowed her tears. "I really hope so."

"It will," said Charlie firmly. "You'll see."

Alice wanted to believe him, but she wasn't sure that she did. She had waited in an empty house like this once before with her baby sisters and their old nurse for company. Her nurse had said that everything would be all right, and then the policeman had come to the door. *There's been an accident...*

A dog barked somewhere on the street. Alice raised her head, and the broad silhouette of a tall man appeared on the road. Her breath caught. "Grandpapa?"

Betty woke, raising her head. "Where is he?"

The light from a tired streetlamp fell over the figure, and Alice knew him instantly. He was stooped and limping, but it was her grandfather.

"Grandpapa." She leaped up from the couch, the little girls tumbling onto the cushions, and ran to the door.

When she ripped the door open, Grandfather had nearly reached her, and she almost screamed at the sight of him. His left eye was puffy and closed, the area around it blotched in black and red and purple. There was blood on his coat and on his knee, long dried and crusty, and he walked with a limp, dragging one foot across the ground.

"Grandpapa," Alice whispered.

"Alice." Grandfather staggered the last steps to her, seized her in one arm and pulled her close to him. "Oh, Alice, my darling. Where are the others?"

"Here, Grandpapa, they're here." Alice returned the embrace even though Grandfather smelled of blood and excrement. "They're all right."

"Oh, thank God," said Grandfather fervently. "Thank God for keeping you all safe. Don't let the little ones see me. I don't want them to be frightened."

He pulled away from Alice and stumbled toward the washroom.

"Grandpapa. Grandpapa." Betty and Hester ran after him.

"Wait a minute, girls. Wait." Alice grabbed their arms. "Grandpapa will come to say hello in a minute." Her heart thudded, and she hoped it was true. His eye looked so awful. And the blood...

"I'll stay with them," said Charlie. "Is he all right?"

"I think so," Alice inhaled. "Charlie, you should really go home. You need your rest."

"I'm fine," Charlie protested. "I can—"

"Please," Alice's voice broke. "Go on home, Charlie."

His shoulders sagged. "All right," he said. "But if you need anything, come and find me."

Alice tried to smile. "Thank you."

She ordered Betty and Hester to stay in the living room while Charlie left, but they ignored her, and she didn't have the strength to stop them. She stumbled into the washroom and froze in the doorway. Grandfather stood hunched over the tin basin, his backbone showing through his wrinkled white skin, which was covered in bruises that throbbed in angry shades of black and red. He splashed water on his face; where it ran down between the curly hairs of his chest, it was red.

Betty screamed.

"Stop that," Alice snapped.

"Grandpapa," Betty wailed.

Hester began to cry.

"Stop it," Alice ordered.

"Leave them be, Allie," said Grandfather tiredly. "They're just frightened. But don't worry, my poppets. I'm all right."

"Go to the bedroom," Alice ordered.

Betty's face twisted with fury, and she grabbed Hester's arm and dragged her off to their bedroom. Alice knew Betty would be angry, but she couldn't bring herself to worry about it. She turned to Grandfather and lifted a clean cloth from the shelf, dipped it in the water and pressed it gently against the bleeding spot on his side. She couldn't tell how deep the wound was. Was she supposed to stop it bleeding, or would the blood wash it clean?

Grandfather winced as Alice touched him.

"I'm sorry," said Alice.

"Where were you, Alice?" Grandfather demanded. "I came home, and this house was empty. There was no sign of any of you. No one knew where you'd gone."

"We couldn't find you," said Alice. "You weren't at the stand."

"So, you went into the *city*." Grandfather slammed a hand down on the wood beside the basin.

Alice drew back, clutching the bloodied rag, and tears prickled her eyes again. Grandfather never yelled, but he'd yelled now, and she was scared.

"I'm sorry." Grandfather took the cloth from her and pressed it to his bleeding side. "I don't want to frighten you, Allie. You've been frightened enough for one night."

"We just wanted to find you," said Alice.

"I know, my poppet," Grandfather sighed. "I was so afraid, too, that something awful had happened to you."

Alice swallowed. "What happened to *you*?"

"Here you are, Grandpapa." She pushed his bowl of porridge toward him. "Nice and warm."

Grandfather jumped, then turned his attention to the bowl. "Ah, yes. Thank you."

"Can we go for a walk when you get home, Grandpapa?" Hester asked.

"No," said Alice. "Grandpapa needs his rest."

"I didn't ask you, Allie," said Hester.

"Girls, girls," Grandfather grunted. "Stop that."

"Well, can we?" said Hester.

Grandfather shook his head. "Not tonight, Hester."

Alice's shoulders sagged, and Betty's habitual pout grew deeper. "But we *never* get to go anywhere anymore," she said. "Never."

"It's so boring," said Hester. "Allie won't read to us."

"I told you, I *can't* read," said Alice. "No one will teach me."

"What about a Christmas tree?" Hester asked. "Can't we go looking for a Christmas tree?"

Ever since the Christmas of the driftwood tree, Grandfather had taken the girls down to the beach as often as he could, and they'd run up and down on the cold sand and searched for another. There never was another, but there was always laughter, which was almost as good. But now Grandfather just shook his head. He still wasn't looking at the girls. "No, not today."

"Then when?" Alice asked.

Grandfather's eyes met hers and filled with tears. "You're staying in this cottage; do you hear me?" he yelled suddenly. "You're not going anywhere."

He rose to his feet and stormed to the door, grabbing his coat on the way.

"Grandpapa," Alice called after him. "Grandpapa, your porridge."

But Grandfather didn't turn around. The entire cottage trembled with the thud as he slammed the door behind him.

※

Henry Pryor felt guilty about shouting at the girls and slamming the door almost immediately after leaving the cottage. His guilt was a weight on his shoulders, but it was nowhere near as heavy as the crushing mass of his terror.

He walked quickly, hands pressed deep into his pockets. The fog lay thickly over London, yellowish and tainted, and the leg he'd broken on the high seas all those years ago throbbed persistently. There'd be snow tonight, he reckoned. There'd have to be snow. Maybe that would finally make the girls happy.

The girls. Henry exhaled, a long, steaming sigh. What was he going to do about them?

"Good morning, Mr. Pryor."

Henry raised his head. Meg Tillman, Charlie's mother, strode purposefully along the path beside him. She carried a huge basket of laundry on her hip, freshly ironed and folded for those who could afford no servants, only a penniless washerwoman.

"Mrs. Tillman." Henry inclined his head.

"I'm glad to see you're still doing all right," said Meg. "Charlie was quite worried about you."

"He's a good lad, that boy," said Henry. "You're doin' right by him."

"Thank you," said Meg. "I'm just glad he could help your girls."

"Yes," Henry sighed heavily. "Me too."

Meg fell into step beside him. "What's on your mind, Henry? You seem so troubled. Are you unwell?"

"No, no. I'm healing just fine," Henry sighed. "It's the girls."

"What about them? Are they all right?"

"They're fine. Bored because I make them stay in that cottage all day. I know it isn't right, you know. I know they should be outside playing and making friends... even going to school, like their mother did."

Meg studied him. "You don't think it's safe."

"I know it's not safe, Meg. Look at what happened to my Annabelle and her husband. And she was a full-grown woman. What could happen to those three poor little girls?" Henry shivered. "Alice is the one I worry about most."

"Alice is a capable girl, and afraid of nothing," said Meg. "She's got a good head on her shoulders."

"Yes, but she's so pretty."

"That she is," Meg chuckled. "I think my Charlie's a bit smitten with her, and I can't blame him. Those blue eyes. Why, she looks so much like her mother."

"She does," said Henry, "and she'll only get prettier. Oh, Meg, you yourself know the dangers of being a pretty girl on these streets."

Meg flinched. Charlie's father was not the man that she was now married to. "Aye, I know," she said softly.

"I couldn't bear something of the sort to happen to Alice."

"I understand," said Meg, "but you can't keep them locked away forever, you know."

"... be back by evening," Grandfather was saying.

Back? Tomorrow was a Sunday, just a couple of days before Christmas. Where would he be going? Grandfather never went anywhere on a Sunday, except to church with the girls.

"Of course, Mr. Pryor," said Meg. "We'll be happy to look after the girls."

He was going somewhere without them? Alice nearly stamped right up to her grandfather and asked him what was going on, but instead, she hesitated in the kitchen, just out of sight. The memory of Grandfather's pale, drawn face and strange behaviour surfaced. Maybe this was her chance to find out what was happening.

"Thank you." Grandfather sounded relieved. "And please thank Charlie again for helping the girls the other night. He's a very good boy."

"Thank you, Mr. Pryor. We're proud of him," said Meg.

Brock just grunted.

"I wish the girls could stay," said Grandfather. "If only more children around here could be like Charlie, then they wouldn't have to go."

Go? Alice's heart thumped sharply. Go where? Why would Grandfather want them to go anywhere?

"I can only imagine that it must be heart-breaking for you," said Meg, "but I know you're doing what you think is best. I couldn't imagine being parted from my Charlie, but I understand why you must let them go."

Alice's body shivered. Why did it sound like they were going somewhere *without* Grandfather? The thought was incomprehensible.

"It's just too dangerous here, Mrs. Tillman," said Grandfather. His words fell like stone slabs, heavy and crushing. "My sister's place in the countryside will be far safer, if I can convince her to take them."

Sister. Alice hadn't even known that Grandfather had a sister at all. Tears rolled down her cheeks, hot and startling. Too dangerous? But it was nearly Christmas. How could they have Christmas without Grandfather?

"In any case, I won't keep you from your home any longer. Thank you for agreeing to look out for them if I'm not home by dark," said Grandfather.

"It's our pleasure, Mr. Tillman," said Brock.

The front door slammed, and Alice panicked. Should she confront Grandfather right now? But then she heard tiny footsteps in the kitchen, and turned to see Hester toddling towards her, sweet-smelling in her crisp white nightie.

Her decision was made instantly. She couldn't talk to Grandfather now, not in front of the smaller girls. They would be shattered if they heard what he was planning.

Her only choice was to somehow convince him to stay.

※

It was the tea and toast in bed that made it hardest to leave.

Henry woke up to the soft padding of bare feet on the wooden floor of his cramped room, the one he'd shared with Angelina when she was still alive. He blinked against the pale glimmer of predawn light through the curtains and saw the slender silhouette of little Alice against the window. She bent over his nightstand and set down a small plate of buttered toast and a mug of hot tea.

Tea in bed on Sundays was nothing new; Alice always did this. But the rich smell of the toast filled the room and made Henry's heart sink.

"Allie?" he mumbled.

She hesitated. "I'm sorry, Grandpapa. I didn't mean to wake you." Her voice was high-pitched and nervous in a way he'd never heard it before. "Take your time. I'll get Betty and Hester ready for church. I've already washed their faces and combed their hair. I'll—"

"Alice, come here." Henry sat up. "Turn up the lantern."

Alice obeyed, filling the room with golden light, and perched on the edge of his bed. Her eyes were round with fear. Henry laid a huge hand on her skinny little arm and stroked it.

"Grandpapa's going away for a little bit today," he said gently. "I'll leave just now, and I'll probably be back by evening, or at the latest, tomorrow morning. Mr. and Mrs. Tillman and Charlie will keep an eye on you. All right?"

"But where are you going, Grandpapa?" Alice whimpered.

Henry didn't want to worry the child without due reason. He wondered if she knew already, but surely, she couldn't. She must have picked up on his nervousness; that was why she had warmed his towel in front of the fire for him last night and put the littler girls to bed early so that he could enjoy a pipe in peace.

"I need to visit my sister in the country. We've been estranged for too long," he said. It was mostly true.

Alice's lip trembled. "Will you come back for Christmas?"

He hoped that the girls would be in their new home by Christmas. "Of course, I will."

"All right." Alice's shoulders sagged slightly. "Can't we come with you?"

"Not this time, poppet." Henry chucked her under the chin. "Thank you for the tea. Run along now and put your sisters back to bed. You might as well have a little lie-in."

Alice slunk out of the room like a kicked dog, and Henry wondered if it was possible to feel worse than he did at that moment.

CHAPTER 5

Alice stood by the window, chewing her thumbnail to a tiny nub. It was early afternoon, and the road was filled with people coming home from church, all dressed up in their Sunday best. She could see their neighbours—mother, father, and two little boys—strolling down the lane, laughing, and joking. The smallest of the boys wore a bright red bowtie with pride, and the father carried three boxes wrapped in brown paper and tied with green ribbons. Christmas presents, Alice supposed.

Last year, she had begged and begged Grandfather to get her some new ribbons for her hair as a Christmas gift. Now, she prayed that she would get to stay here with him and her sisters for Christmas. All she wanted was for them to be together.

"Alliiiiiiie," Betty whined. "You said you'd play with us."

"I will," said Alice, "but not right now."

"You've been saying that for *hours*." Hester grabbed her skirt, yanking it sharply. "We want you to *playyyyyy*." Her high-pitched tone grated sharply on Alice's nerves.

Alice gritted her teeth. "I wish you'd stop whining."

"We're not whining," snapped Betty.

"We want to go outside," Hester complained. "We want to play a game. We're so bored."

"We *are* bored," Betty moaned. "When's Grandpapa coming back?"

Fear boiled into anger in Alice's chest. "Soon," she snapped, "and he's going to send all of you to bed without any dinner if you don't start behaving yourselves."

"No," Hester wailed. "I don't want to go to bed early." She covered her face with her hands and wept.

"Stop that," yelled Alice.

"You stop it." Betty shouted back. "You're so awful. Why can't you just be nice?"

"Why can't you just be—bigger?" Alice demanded.

Betty glared at her and put her arms around Hester, who sobbed louder. Her cries cut through Alice's aching head. She covered her ears with her hands and stumbled out toward the back garden, Betty and Hester trailing along behind her.

"Why are you so mean today?" Hester sobbed.

"That's just the way she is, Hestie," said Betty. "She's just an ugly person."

"I'm *not*," Alice shouted.

She reached the garden and stumbled into the cool, clear winter air. Real snow had fallen in the night; it sparkled undisturbed where the lawn had been and draped the bare branches of the plane trees. Alice gulped a few deep breaths of the refreshing air. She needed to get dinner on the stove for Grandfather. She would make him his favorite soup. Then maybe he'd forget he'd spoken to his mysterious sister in the country, and the girls wouldn't have to leave.

Hester plucked at her skirt again. "Up," she moaned, holding out her arms.

"Why are you being such a baby today?" Alice demanded. "Walk with your own two feet."

She brushed past Betty and the still-wailing Hester and strode toward the kitchen.

"Why won't you just play with us?" Betty demanded. "We just want to play some tag. Come on, Alice. Stop being horrid."

"I'm not going to play," said Alice.

"But we're *booooooored*," Hester howled.

"I'm bored, too. Anyone would be bored stuck with the two of you," Alice shouted.

She regretted the words the instant they left her mouth. Hester stumbled back like she'd been slapped, her eyes growing huge.

Alice deflated. "I'm sorry, Hestie."

"You hate us," Hester whimpered. She tore herself away from Betty, wailing, and ran to the front door. "You hate us."

"Hestie," Alice yelled. "Get back here."

She knew she shouldn't have yelled, but her panic rose in her more quickly than she could stop it when Hester's fat fingers twisted the doorknob and the little girl sprinted out onto the road.

"*Hestie.*" Alice screamed.

She raced after the child, but those little legs were surprisingly fast, and Hester was already passing the neighbours' house. Betty hovered in the doorway, ready to come after them.

"Stay there," Alice ordered.

Betty froze, but Hester was still running, heading down the path that led to the docks. Alice thought of the scary old woman, and her gut twisted. Had she returned? Could she catch Hester before the old hag saw her?

"Hestie, please, I didn't mean it," Alice called, swinging her arms to run faster. "Please stop. Stop."

She caught her at the end of the lane, right where it forked to the docks, and flung her arms around Hester's body. Hester screamed and wailed, and Alice lifted her off her feet, kicking and crying.

"You hate us," Hester sobbed. "You hate us."

"I don't hate you," Alice panted. "I'm sorry. I'm so sorry."

But Hester still cried all the way home, and Alice felt the eyes of every person she passed locked onto her in accusing judgment. She kept her head down as she bundled Hester back into the house, pulled the door closed and locked it.

"Don't you shout at her, Allie," said Betty hotly.

"I'm not going to shout," said Alice, exhausted. "I was going to make some tea."

Betty deflated slightly, but her eyes were still accusing as she wrapped her arms around her sister.

"Let's have some nice hot tea," said Alice, "and then I'll play with you." She would do anything if it would stop them from screaming.

There was no playing. When they'd finished their cups of tea, Betty and Hester fell asleep with their heads in Alice's lap. Alice stared out of the living room window at the now-empty street and willed Grandfather to come home.

But as twilight fell over the grey sea, there was still no sign of him.

※

Henry's shadow stretched out in front of him as he walked, as ragged and endless as this day had been. The sun was setting at his back, and he was still miles from home. Still miles from a solution, if there was one to be found at all, and the ominous chafing on his left heel had turned to the exquisite pain of a blister. It was nothing compared to the aching fatigue in all his muscles.

Henry ignored the exhaustion and the pain. He kept his head down, focusing on his worn and tired boots as he dragged them across the thin layer of snow that covered this section of country lane, labouring up to the top of a hill.

When he reached the top, he paused, breathing heavily, and leaned against the gnarled, leafless oak that grew there. At the bottom of the hill, at the end of the winding little street, lay Edgeword, slumbering beneath the grey smoke of its chimneys and the shadow of its little steeple.

Number four, the old woman in the last village had told him, *on the end of the street, next to the church. That's where Mary Hardin lives.*

Finding her had been almost impossible. Henry trudged down the hill, turning up the collar of his coat against the cold. He

"Please, Mary," he said. "I didn't know they'd sent you away. I couldn't stop them. I wasn't there."

Mary stopped. Her cold eyes met his; Eleanor all but cowered behind her.

"That's right, Henry," she said bitterly. "You weren't there. You *never* were."

Her words cut Henry to the quick. He'd started out as a cabin boy; he'd spent most of her childhood on the high seas.

"Every time I hoped for my brother to come and save me, there was no one," said Mary. "Of course, I had to turn to Roger. He was the one who was *there*."

"I'm sorry," said Henry, meaning it.

Mary laughed. "A likely story. If you were sorry, you would have come to find me twenty years ago, not now."

Henry swallowed. How could he explain the whirlwind of those twenty years to Mary? He'd already been married to Angelina when Mary disappeared, and it had been shortly after that that their daughter came along. Then the wedding, the grandbabies, Angelina's death... and the loss of his daughter and his precious son-in-law. And the girls.

The girls. Henry squared his shoulders, reminded of his mission.

"I'm here now," he said. "May I come in?"

Mary watched him with narrowed eyes. "All right."

She led him into a farmhouse that was just as cosy on the inside; warm, clean, and bright, with a few ornaments on the mantelpiece, lace curtains on the windows. It had few luxuries and no servants, but it smelled of freshly baked bread. The living room was carpeted and had comfortable couches arranged around a huge, crackling hearth, with a towering Christmas tree in the corner, so tall that its tip was a little squashed by the ceiling. It was wrapped in ribbons and hung with oranges and gingerbread men, with a few humble gifts lying at its feet.

Henry felt a stab of guilt. He hadn't even gone looking for a tree with the girls yet, the way he always did, even though they all knew that they weren't going to find one.

A paunchy, ruddy man sat in an armchair by the fire, slippers held out to the flame. He glared up with rheumy eyes as Mary, Eleanor and Henry came in.

"Henry, this is Roger," said Mary. "My husband." There was a tattered pride in the words.

Roger raised a dark brown bottle to Henry.

"Roger, this is my brother," said Mary.

Roger's expression darkened. "What do you want?"

"My forgiveness, I suppose," said Mary snidely. She sat on the couch; Eleanor perched beside her, and Henry stayed standing.

"No," said Henry.

Mary stared at him, her face cold and frozen.

"I'm not here for your forgiveness, Mary," he said quietly. "I know I don't deserve it." Perhaps that was the real reason why he'd never come in all these years, he thought. "I'm here because I have nowhere else to turn."

Roger grunted. "Likely story."

"Shut up, Roger," said Mary.

Roger glowered at her but said nothing.

Henry inhaled. "I need your help."

Mary laughed. "My *help*? My *help*? I needed *your* help when Ma and Pa threw me out on my ear just because of the man I loved, Henry. The cheek of it."

"I have three granddaughters," said Henry suddenly.

Mary's mouth snapped shut.

Eleanor leaned forward, her eyes shining. "How old are they?"

"Little Hester is only five." Henry smiled despite himself. "Betty is six, and sweet Alice is ten."

"I'm fourteen," said Eleanor.

Henry glanced in surprise at Mary, and the sudden tears in her eyes told him exactly why there was only the one child.

"Where's their mother?" Mary asked sharply.

"Dead," said Henry. "Their father and grandmother too. I'm trying to raise them, but it's just too dangerous in London. The biggest girl, my Alice... she's growing very pretty. So pretty." He lowered his gaze. "She's not safe. None of them will be when they start to grow up. I need somewhere for them to stay, somewhere far from those kinds of scoundrels."

Mary barked a laugh. "So, you thought you'd palm them off on me."

"I just want my girls to be safe, Mary," said Henry. "I would do anything to make that happen. Anything," he added fiercely.

Mary rose to her feet. "Get out."

"Please, Mary," Henry held out a hand.

"I don't believe your cheek." cried Mary. "You abandoned me when I needed you, and now you waltz in here wanting me to take in three waifs that I've never even met."

"They're not waifs." Henry boomed.

It was the first time he'd raised his voice, and silence fell suddenly on the group.

Henry forced his tone to be gentle. "They're not waifs," he said again. "They're beautiful, hardworking, well-mannered little girls, and they'll be a credit to you. What's more, they're not homeless. I'll send money every month, cover all their expenses."

Roger leaned forward. "How much money?"

Henry had thought long and hard about the figure. It was every penny he could spare. He named it, and Roger whistled softly.

Mary folded her arms. "Ten, six, and five, you say."

"Would you pay the same for just two?" Roger demanded.

The thought of splitting up the girls made Henry's heart squeeze, but maybe it could work. If he kept Hester, that would buy him a little time while she grew up.

"Just the two bigger ones," Roger added.

"Well..." Henry began.

"No," said Mary suddenly. Her eyes darted to Eleanor and then to her own midriff, as though contemplating her barren womb. "No, I want all of them."

"What?" said Roger.

Henry swallowed, hope springing in him. Mary was angry now, but the way she said it... *I want all of them*. Maybe she envisioned having the house full of children she'd always wanted. Though she would never love him again, maybe she would love those girls.

"You heard me," said Mary acerbically. "I want the little ones. I want them all."

"But—" Roger began.

"I won't pay for only two," said Henry quickly. "It has to be all three."

Roger scowled. "It's not enough."

"Shut up," said Mary again.

Henry blinked, startled that Roger allowed her to talk to him in that way, or perhaps more startled that Mary would speak to her husband that way. Angelina would never. Then again, he thought, watching Roger swig from a dark bottle, perhaps he had been a different husband to Angelina than Roger was to Mary.

"So you'll take them?" said Henry hesitantly.

Mary's jaw set.

"Mama—" Eleanor began pleadingly.

"Yes," said Mary. "I'll take them. Bring them tomorrow."

Henry's heart swooped. "Tomorrow? That's Christmas Eve."

"Do you want me to take them or not?" Mary snapped.

Henry swallowed. "I do. Please. I'll bring them."

"Good," said Mary. "You know the way out."

Henry trudged out into the snow with a heavy heart. He stood in front of the farmhouse and gazed at the little street, bordered by cottages and farmland. The choir in the church was now singing "I Heard the Bells on Christmas Day".

Then rang the bells more loud and deep

God is not dead, nor does He sleep

Though long shall fail to rise the veil

Of peace on earth, goodwill to man.

Henry breathed the fresh air deeply. This would break his heart, he knew. But if his girls could grow up in a place like this, safe and well, loved and happy, then it was worth having his heart broken.

***

It was dark.

Alice had bathed the two little girls and given them dinner, not knowing what else to do. They'd eaten heaping spoonsful of the butternut soup that Grandfather liked so much. Alice had eaten an extra small portion to make sure that there was plenty left for Grandfather. Maybe, just maybe, it would still change his mind.

Or maybe he was lying dead on a road somewhere, crushed just like Mama and Papa.

She watched as Hester happily swallowed the last mouthful of her soup and scraped her spoon around the bowl for more. Alice's cheery smile, pasted into place by sheer willpower, was clearly working. The two smaller girls were fairly settled this evening. Maybe she'd even get them off to sleep. She'd told them that Grandfather was visiting a friend and would only be back by morning; that a fairy had come and told her the news. Hester was fascinated by fairies, so she'd spent the rest of the afternoon spinning wild stories about them. It was exhausting, but at least they weren't whining anymore.

The knock at the door made Alice jump. Betty looked up. "Grandpapa's early."

Alice's heart leaped within her. She flew out of her seat and ran to the door, aching with joy and terror. "Grandpapa." she called.

"Grandpapa." Hester ran after her, squealing happily.

Alice grabbed the door and wrenched it open, but her smile died on her lips. There was no towering, shaggy old pirate at the door. Instead, it was just Charlie, small and slender, his eyes gentle as ever.

"Sorry," he said. "It's just me."

"Charlie," squealed Hester happily, hugging his knees. Betty followed suit, and Charlie's laugh was warm and happy enough that it nearly made Alice feel a little better.

"I've come to see if Mr. Pryor is home yet," Charlie explained, hugging the girls back.

"Not yet." Alice cleared her throat. "A fairy told me he's only coming in the morning."

Charlie met her eyes and understood. "Ah, I see. Fairies are never wrong, you know."

Hester giggled. "They're very pretty too."

"*So* pretty." Charlie bent down and swung the little girl onto his shoulders. "Why don't you come home with me for the night?"

"It's all right," said Alice. "We don't want to impose."

"Yes," squealed Hester, delighted.

"Yes, yes." Betty bounced up and down.

Charlie smiled. "Ma and Pa suggested it. You won't impose. We don't want to leave you in that cold empty cottage, do we?"

Alice looked over her shoulder and shivered. Although the fire still leaped in the kitchen hearth, Charlie was right. The cottage had never felt colder or emptier.

"All right," she said.

"Good," said Charlie. "Come along, then."

He strode jauntily down the street, Hester bouncing on his shoulders, Betty holding his hand. Alice trailed along behind, head hanging.

It was just a few minutes' walk to the Tillman cottage, which was much smaller and more tumbledown than Grandfather's. It smelled faintly of mould as Charlie led the girls inside. His baby sisters were already sleeping; the tiny kitchen contained only Meg and Brock, who were talking in hushed voices until the girls came in, when they fell suddenly silent.

"Hello, girls." Meg smiled, but her eyes were strained.

Brock grunted and left the room.

"I'm sorry, Mrs. Tillman," said Alice. "I... we... we already ate. We just... we only need a blanket to share. That's all."

"Don't you worry one bit, little ones." Meg hoisted herself slowly to her feet. "I've put a rug in front of the fire for you. You'll be safe and warm until your grandfather comes to get you."

But when Alice lay on the hard rug, tucked between her sisters, staring at the flames as they licked over a few pieces of damp wood, she wondered if Grandfather was coming back at all. If he wanted to send them away, then why would he return? Maybe he would just leave them here.

Maybe they would always be alone.

"That all sounds lovely, poppet," said Grandfather. "Thank you."

"Tomorrow's Christmas," Alice added. "Maybe this afternoon we can go looking for a tree."

Grandfather cleared his throat. "Yes, perhaps."

They reached the house, and Alice turned to go to the kitchen, but Grandfather stopped her.

"Girls," he said, "there's something I must tell you. Let's go into the living room."

Alice's heart plummeted through the floor. She froze in place; suddenly she wanted to run away or scream or hit somebody. Anything other than walking into that living room and hearing the news that made tears shimmer in her grandfather's eyes. Seeing him on the brink of crying made Alice feel like the universe was melting.

"Please," Grandfather said quietly.

No amount of shouting could have coaxed her into that living room, but the quiet word from Grandfather did.

Grandfather sat down on his ancient, patched, and tattered armchair, the one whose arms had two smoothly worn marks in exactly the places where Grandfather rested his elbows exactly as he was doing now. He peered over his hands at the three girls as Alice, Betty and Hester sat all in a row on the couch.

Betty and Hester squirmed and giggled, heedless of the agony in Grandfather's eyes, but Alice sat still. Maybe if she didn't move or breathe then time wouldn't pass, and Grandfather wouldn't say what she feared he was going to say.

"Girls," he said, "I have good news for you."

Alice's heart leaped, and she leaned forward. *Good news.* They were going to stay. The tears in her grandfather's eyes were tears of relief.

"You're going to a wonderful new home," he said.

Alice's heart slammed into the floor like a dropped weight. "Wh–what?"

"You're going to stay with my sister and her husband and her lovely daughter Eleanor," said Grandfather. "They live on a beautiful farm in the country, and you won't believe it, but they have the most wonderful Christmas tree I've ever seen."

"A Christmas tree," Hester squealed. "Are there any presents?"

"Lots of presents, my poppet," said Grandfather.

Alice sat absolutely still. Tears streaked down her face.

"How old is Eleanor?" asked Betty.

"She's fourteen," said Grandfather. "Old enough to teach you girls everything you need to know about girlhood." He laughed. "And the fields. Their village is lovely, but the fields are even better. Endless room to run and play."

FAYE GODWIN

"You mean we'll get to play outside?" Hester breathed.

"As much as you want, poppet," said Grandfather.

Hester squealed and clapped her hands. Alice shivered where she sat.

"How long will we be staying with them, Grandfather?" she croaked.

Grandfather's face stilled, and the smaller girls' giggles faded abruptly.

"For always, my poppet," he said. "You're going to stay with Mary and Roger and Eleanor the way you've stayed with me. They're going to take care of you, and you'll be safe there. No one will ever chase you or try to steal you again."

Betty and Hester were silent. Alice swallowed again and again, trying to choke down the lump in her throat that threatened to suffocate her.

"Maybe you'll even learn to read," said Grandfather. "Eleanor can read. She might teach you. Then even on rainy days when you can't play outside, you could be curled up around a book. Doesn't that sound just lovely?"

"Playing outside," said Betty, her eyes gleaming. "All the time, Grandpapa?"

"All the time, my poppet," said Grandfather.

Betty giggled with excitement.

Alice swallowed again, but she couldn't stop the tears that came faster and faster. Grandfather rose to his feet. "Betty, Hester, why don't you go to the kitchen and look on the kitchen table? I brought us a lovely loaf of country bread for breakfast."

The two little girls tumbled from the room, and Grandfather held out his arms. Alice flew into them. She pressed her face into his jacket and breathed the ocean smell, and her tears cascaded into his shirt as he held her.

"Please," she sobbed. "Please, Grandpapa, I'll never do anything naughty ever again. I'll keep them in the cottage. I'll do everything perfectly. Please, please, don't send me away."

"Alice, poppet." Grandfather knelt the way he used to do when she was a very little girl, his hands resting on her shoulders, his eyes seeking hers. "I know that you don't now understand, but one day you will. One day you will know that I didn't do this because of anything you did, but only because I love you, and I want the best for you."

"The best for me is to be with you, Grandpapa," Alice sobbed.

"I know you think that, my poppet, I know." Grandfather hugged her again. "But I need you to trust me and believe me now when I tell you that this is for your own good. This is the only way."

Alice pressed her face into his neck and sobbed, but she didn't beg or plead. She didn't have the words.

Alice exhaled slowly and let her hand fall to her side. "He doesn't need to come in, Hestie." She took Hester's hand. "We're just fine, aren't we, Betty?"

Betty nodded slowly.

"Goodbye, my poppets." Grandfather rested his hand on the top of Alice's head.

"Bye-bye, Grandpapa," said Hester.

"Merry Christmas," said Betty.

Grandfather looked at Alice for a long, long moment, but she couldn't muster a word. Not even when he turned and walked away.

MARY HARDIN HAD eyes that were blue like Charlie's, but that was where the resemblance ended.

Any hope that Alice had had shriveled up and died in her chest the moment she looked into those icy blue eyes. Mary swept the three girls with them, and a sneer quirked the corner of her lip.

"You must be Henry's granddaughters," she said.

"Yes, Mrs. Hardin," said Alice carefully. She held out an envelope that Grandfather had given her. Oh, Grandfather. It still smelled like him, and she suddenly didn't want to let it go.

Mary plucked it from her hand. "Didn't know the old coot could read."

"H-his bookkeeper wrote it for him," Alice croaked.

"Ah. I see." Mary's eyes flashed. "I suppose you'd better come in."

Hester giggled and pulled free from Alice. She ran to Mary and flung her chubby arms around the older woman's knees, hugging her. "Mary," she giggled. "Mama Mary."

Mary stiffened, and Alice lunged, ready to grab Hester and pull her back. But then the woman's eyes softened, and she wrapped her arms around Hester.

"That's right, dear," she said. "I'm your Mama Mary now."

Betty inched nearer. "I don't remember my mama," she said.

"That's all right," said Mary. "You have a new one now." She smiled, and her eyes were suddenly much kinder.

Alice stepped forward and opened her mouth, but Mary's eyes narrowed, freezing her in place.

"You will call me Mrs. Hardin," she growled. "Can you cook?"

Alice swallowed. "Yes."

"Good. Then go to the kitchen and help Eleanor with peeling potatoes for Christmas dinner," said Mary sharply.

Alice didn't know where the kitchen was, but she didn't dare say so. She could only watch as Mary hustled the two smaller girls into a drawing room filled with decorations and light. In contrast, the hallway felt very cold, very grey, and very, very alone.

PART II

Alice knelt by the grate of the kitchen fire, polishing it. Her knees ached from the pressure of the cold stone floor, but at least the coal stove in the corner provided some warmth. Eleanor stirred onions in a huge cast-iron pan on the stove and shot baleful looks at the two smaller girls.

"Is the gingerbread dough all right, Mama?" she asked in the high-pitched little-girl voice that she used every time she spoke to her mother, even though she was sixteen now.

Mary didn't look up. "Oh yes, Ellie dear, it's fine."

Eleanor's face fell. She shot another glare at Betty and Hester, then turned back to the pan.

Alice bit back a sigh as she scrubbed the last piece of the grate and tossed her cleaning tools into a pail. She rose to her feet and wiped her hands on a rag. "It's all clean now, Mrs. Hardin."

"Good," said Mary, enthralled by the gingerbread man that Hester had just cut. "Just in time to go to the grocer's."

Alice glanced out of the window. Snowflakes swirled against the glass, thudding and hissing; the wind howled around the corners of the farmhouse.

Mary raised her head. "What are you waiting for, Alice? Go on."

"Yes, Mrs. Hardin." Alice ducked her head, took the shopping basket from the table with the few coins in the bottom, and hurried out of the front door.

It had taken her weeks, when she'd first come here, to notice just how peerlessly blue the sky was or how wonderfully crisp the air was compared to the polluted air on London's docks. Today, though, the sky was a swirl of grey, and snowflakes beat against Alice's face as she walked. She kept her head down, shivering in the threadbare coat that no longer fit her, and shuffled to the grocer's shop at the end of the street.

Her fingers were frozen when she pushed the door open, jangling the little bell over the door. The shop was empty, and the old widow behind the counter looked up in shock.

"Why, Allie," she said, "what are you doing here in this weather?"

Alice shook the snow from her shoulders and shut the door behind her. "Mrs. Hardin sent me for some things, Mrs. Porter." She held out the handwritten list that Mary had given her.

Mrs. Porter sighed. "Two years you've been with her this Christmas, and she still makes you call her by that name, doesn't she? While your little sisters call her 'Mama Mary' and her own daughter grows more and more resentful by the day."

Alice cleared her throat. "I think one of the things she wants will be potatoes."

Mrs. Porter brightened. "Ah, potatoes, is it?" She looked at the list. "Why, Allie dear, you're learning. Potatoes indeed."

Mrs. Porter was a bony old hag of a creature, but her little black button eyes shone with kindness. Alice felt her heart loosen a little in the old widow's presence. She laughed. "Do you have time for any reason today, Mrs. Porter?"

Mrs. Porter chuckled. "Look at the weather, child. Nobody's going to buy groceries today." She pulled a newspaper from under the counter and held it out. "You start with page three while I pack your groceries."

"Thank you." Alice smiled and took the paper. She squinted down at the first headline on the page that Mrs. Porter had indicated. "Farmer," she began, tracing the word with her fingers. "Farmer, sells, bull, for."

"Good," said Mrs. Porter, putting some tomatoes into the basket. "And the next word?"

Alice squinted. "Res... Rek... Reo..."

"Record," said Mrs. Porter.

"*Record*. Farmer sells bull for record... price?" Alice attempted.

Mrs. Porter beamed. "Perfect. Well done, dear. Keep going."

Alice stumbled her way through the first sentence of the article. Her voice gained confidence as she struggled through the second but didn't need any help to get to the end. When she finished the sentence, flushed and triumphant, Mrs. Porter applauded.

"Look at you go," she said. "You're reading like a little schoolgirl."

"Can we practice writing?" Alice asked eagerly.

Mrs. Porter put the full basket down on the counter. "Of course, dear, if you have time."

Alice's shoulders sagged. She'd just learned to form the basic letters, but it had been more than a fortnight since she'd had the chance to practice with Mrs. Porter.

"I'm sorry." Alice laid down the newspaper. "I really have to be getting back."

Mrs. Porter's mouth turned down in sympathy. "Chores waiting for you, dear?"

"We're getting ready for Christmas. There's a lot to do," said Alice.

"It's good for children to pull their weight, but, well, seems to me that you pull more weight than necessary."

Alice shrugged. "I'm glad that my sisters are happy."

"That's as may be, dear, but you and Eleanor don't look very happy."

"Maybe not." Alice fingered the paper. "I wish that I could teach my little sisters to read, though. I don't know if Mary can. If she does, she hasn't started teaching them."

"Why don't you?" asked Mrs. Porter.

"I can't. I hardly have a moment with my sisters anymore; Mary takes them everywhere. Their room is right next to her own, and Eleanor and I sleep all the way at the end of the hall." Alice brushed a hand over her hair. "I should go."

Mrs. Porter sighed. "Be safe, dear."

"Thank you," said Alice. She took the basket and hastened into the blowing snow, ignoring the cheerful wreath hanging on the shop door behind her. It had been a long time since the sight of bright red holly berries had engendered anything except pure dread in Alice's heart.

THE AIR in the little dining room was tight with tension. Alice kept her head down and her eyes focused on the excellent soup, which she'd made with a little begrudging help from Eleanor. It was butternut soup. Hungry though she was, Alice struggled to swallow each bite. It was like sawdust in her mouth; she hadn't been able to eat butternut soup since the Christmas that Grandfather had left them here.

Eleanor sat beside Alice, her face a black cloud as she picked at her soup. Roger kept his head down and said nothing. It was Hester's cheerful little voice that cut through the dark atmosphere.

"We made gingerbread men today, Mr. Hardin," she said.

Unlike Mary, Roger had never let anyone call him anything other than Mr. Hardin. Even Eleanor had fallen into the habit of doing this from time to time, Alice had noticed.

Roger didn't acknowledge a word Hester said. He broke off a piece of bread, dunked it in his soup and ate it without looking up.

"They're so pretty. They're going to look lovely on the tree," said Hester.

"Yes," said Betty. "Did you find a tree for us yet, Mr. Hardin?"

Mary beamed proudly at the two girls. Roger glowered briefly at Betty, then returned to his plate. "No."

"I'm sure Roger will find the time to cut down a tree for us tomorrow, dear," said Mary, patting Betty's hand. "Why don't you have some more bread?"

"There's a blizzard outside, Mary," Roger snapped. "Why would I cut down a stupid Christmas tree in this weather?"

Mary's eyes narrowed. "It's nearly Christmas. You're late."

"I'll do it when I want to do it, woman," Roger yelled.

Alice flinched. Betty and Hester stared at him, and Hester whimpered.

"Now look what you've done," said Mary.

Roger sighed. "I'm sorry." He returned to his meal.

Alice swallowed another spoonful of soup, choking it down reluctantly despite the hunger that gnawed at the pit of her stomach. Eleanor had been responsible for cutting the bread, and Alice had gotten only a tiny piece.

"I finished my piece of sewing today," said Eleanor. "I'm almost done with my new dress, Mama."

Mary was busily adding more bread to Betty's plate. "Oh, that's nice."

"Would you like to see it after supper?" Eleanor asked. "I think I could use your help with one of the seams."

"Don't be ridiculous, Eleanor," snapped Mary. "You know how to sew a seam by now."

Eleanor lowered her head. "Yes, Mrs. Ha— Yes, Mary."

Alice edged a little nearer to Eleanor. "I could help you with the seam, if you—"

"You'll stay away from my dress," Eleanor yelled. "It's mine, do you hear me? *Mine.*"

"Alice, stop bothering Eleanor," Roger snapped.

"Yes, Mr. Hardin. I'm sorry," said Alice.

"You'd think that you would be more grateful for everything this family does for you," Roger spat.

Mary huffed. "As if. You're a greedy little wench."

"She was just saying that she wants a new dress, Mama," said Eleanor. "As if the one she has isn't good enough for her already."

"I don't," said Alice quickly. "I never said that."

"I heard her complaining about it," said Eleanor. "All the time. 'Why is my dress so tatty?' she keeps saying."

"No, I love my dress," said Alice hastily, plucking at a threadbare sleeve.

"Ungrateful wench," spat Roger. "You're not even touching the food that I've given you."

Alice had picked the butternuts, peeled them, and cooked them, but she dared not say that. She scooped up a hasty spoonful and choked it down.

"What's the matter with you, Alice?" Mary demanded. "You're always in such a mood. Why do you always have to bring everyone else down?"

"I don't mean to," said Alice, tears rolling down her cheeks.

"She's crying again, Mama Mary," said Betty.

"Please, I'm not trying to be difficult." Alice wiped her tears and swallowed. "I just—I—"

"You're spoiled, that's what you are," said Roger. "Greedy and ungrateful."

"No," Alice sobbed. "I'm not. I just— I just miss Grandpapa, every day and every night, all of the time. I can't stop missing him." She covered her face with her hands and wept.

Eleanor folded her arms and huffed. Betty glared, and Roger looked away, his jaw tight with fury. Hester didn't look up from her soup. Alice weeping over supper was nothing new to her.

"Alice, you are such a baby," said Mary. "I'm so tired of hearing about how much you miss your grandfather. It's been two years."

"I haven't seen him even once in all that time," Alice sobbed.

"That's because he never loved you," said Mary acidly. "He just left you here and made you my problem. Now eat your soup and stop that ridiculous noise."

"It's not true," Alice wept. "It's not true. I know he wants to see us. I just wish I could see him again."

Roger sighed. "Ever since you brought this child here, woman, we haven't been able to have a happy Christmas. She only mopes more and more each year."

"Shut up," Mary yelled.

Roger gritted his teeth and went back to his soup.

Alice dried her eyes as well as she could. "Please, Mary," she whispered. "If I could just go and visit him, just once…"

"This again." Eleanor rolled her eyes.

"I'm not talking about this with you again, Alice," snapped Mary. "Who would do your work while you're away? Who would pay for you to go there? No. There will be absolutely no visiting."

"I'll make money. I'll find a way," Alice protested. "Please just let me see my grandpapa again."

Mary flew to her feet. "That's it. I'm sick to the death of you whining about your grandfather all the time, especially over Christmas."

"If I could see him—" Alice began.

"Enough." Roger slammed a hand down on the table, making all of the soup bowls jump. "Can a man not enjoy food in his own house anymore?"

Alice burst into tears, sobbing hard.

"Go to your bedroom," Roger snapped. "Don't come out until your morning chores."

Alice stumbled to her feet and headed out of the room.

"Answer me, girl," Roger roared. "Is that understood?"

Alice's tears dripped down her cheeks. "Yes, Mr. Hardin."

"Now get out of my sight," Roger snarled.

Before she fled the room, Alice caught a last glimpse of the triumph in Eleanor's eyes, the fierceness in Betty's, and the total indifference of her little sister as Hester continued to pick happily at her soup without a care in the world.

"Alice," Mary called.

Alice froze. She sat in the kitchen in a small wooden chair, trying to enjoy the tiny pool of tepid sunlight that filtered in through the window, sparkling on the snowbound landscape outside. Roger's shirt lay in her lap; she was halfway through sewing a patch onto the back.

"Alice," Mary called again.

Alice swallowed nervously. It wasn't that Mary was calling for her in an angry tone—quite the opposite. If Mary had shrieked, Alice would have set the sewing aside and run upstairs the way she did twenty times a day. Instead, there was something strange about Mary's voice, something almost sweet.

What was happening?

"Alice, dear," Mary called. "Where are you?"

Alice forced her legs to work. She laid the shirt on the kitchen table and made for the stairs. "I'm coming, Mrs. Hardin."

Her hands shook as she reached the landing and pushed open the door to Mary's bedroom. The room was large and airy, with a cheerful fire in the grate and a bed strewn with pillows. The window overlooked the beautiful fields, wrapped in ribbons of dark stone walls, quiet and still under the sparkling snow. Alice could see the steam train that passed by the village chuffing along, trailed by a plume of steam as white as the snow.

Mary's armchair was by the window, and she sat in it now, holding a piece of paper. Her eyes were filled with tears.

"What's wrong?" asked Alice. "What's happened?"

"Oh, my poor little Alice, I'm so sorry," said Mary. "I have very bad news. Come and sit here with me, darling."

Alice's skin crawled at Mary's syrupy tone. Something had to be wrong for her great-aunt to address her in that way; she didn't think Mary had ever spoken so kindly to her. She edged nearer.

"Sit, Alice, sit," said Mary, gesturing to the wooden chair opposite her.

Alice perched on it and tried to get a look at the paper in Mary's hand, but it was turned away from her so that she couldn't even see the outline of the words through the back of the page.

"Mrs. Hardin, what's happened?" Alice whispered.

"I'm so sorry to have to tell you this, dear," said Mary, "but it's your grandfather."

The image of Grandfather filled Alice's mind. His big laugh. His ocean eyes. The tenderness of his gnarled old hands, rough though they were from years of wrestling with tarry ropes on the open ocean.

"Grandpapa?" Alice whispered. Fresh tears rolled down her cheeks.

"Yes," said Mary. "I'm so sorry, dear, but he's dead."

The way she said it—*he's dead*—slammed like a door in Alice's soul. Her knees turned to water, and she collapsed on the chair, doubled over, wheezing with shock and agony. She knew instantly that it was true. The only thing that could possibly have kept Grandfather from her for two long years was death.

"No," she sobbed out, tears rushing down her cheeks. "No... no... Grandpapa."

"Yes, it's very sad," said Mary, patting her lightly on the back. "But there's nothing we can do about it, is there?"

Alice's mind flooded with questions. How could this have happened? How could such a titanic figure leave this world? She sat up, tried to sob out one of her questions, but none of them would come. Between the lump in her throat and the shock in her mind, they grew scrambled, and the syllables came out in meaningless chunks.

"Now, now, none of that," said Mary briskly. "Chin up, that's the spirit. Henry wouldn't want you to carry on like this, would he?"

Alice didn't know; all she knew was that he was dead, but Mary must be right. She swallowed her tears as well as she could.

"Now wash your face and carry on with your sewing," said Mary. "It's all over now."

It was all over now. The tiny scrap of hope that Alice had had left, the one that longed for Grandfather to come and get her, was crushed. There was nothing left. She was stuck here. Her life was reduced to this now, forever.

She would rather have been trapped in that cottage for a thousand lifetimes with Grandfather and Betty and Hester and Charlie than survive another day like this.

"Go on," said Mary.

Somehow Alice was standing and wobbling to the door even though her body felt as though it was no longer tethered to the world. Her hand was on the doorknob when Mary said, "Oh, and Alice?"

She turned, saying nothing; her throat felt too raw to speak.

Mary's eyes were steel. "That's the last I want to hear about your grandfather ever again," she said. "He's gone now. There's no reason to talk about him."

Alice stared at her, uncomprehending. Was she meant to act as though her grandfather had never existed?

"Do you understand?" Mary demanded. "If I hear another word from you about him, you'll disgrace his memory. He doesn't want you to mope around missing him. He wants you to get on with your life. I won't let you dishonour my brother. Do you hear me?"

Alice looked into the cold and empty eyes and nodded once.

"Good," said Mary. "Now go."

Alice went. Went forth into a world that felt hollow and frozen, a grandfather-shaped hole blasted in the fabric of reality.

CHAPTER 8

ALICE WOKE when a pillow slammed over her face. She flailed for a moment, panic gripping her, thinking that she was being suffocated. But the pillow fell easily to the floor.

"Stop that," Eleanor hissed from the narrow bed beside hers. "Stop it. I can't sleep a wink with you carrying on so." She rolled angrily onto her other side and ripped her blankets up over her shoulder.

Alice lay still, trying to breathe as quietly as possible, steam curling in the air. There was no fire in their room; they had to rely on the warmth radiating from the fires in the master bedroom and the room that the littler girls shared. There were many nights that Alice longed for the winters when she'd shared a bed with her two sisters. Tonight was not one of them. Her sheets were drenched with sweat, and her heart galloped like a loose horse in her chest.

She'd been dreaming of Grandfather. In her dream, he had been laughing as he walked up from the beach, carrying their driftwood Christmas tree on his back. Then, as he walked, the ground beneath his feet turned to quicksand. He sank below it, still laughing, and no matter how fast Alice ran, she only grew farther and farther away from him as she strove to reach him.

The memory of his laugh—still so rich and mellow in her mind—was enough to make her sob again.

Eleanor sat up. "Get out," she hissed.

Alice stared at her.

"Get out of this room," Eleanor ordered.

The fury in her eyes scared Alice. She scrambled to her feet, blankets still wrapped around her, and trailed into the hallway.

It was chilly here, a draft blowing in through the hall window that never closed properly. Alice stumbled up to it, twitched the curtains aside, and gazed into the fields beyond. The wintry night was still and perfect. The stars were brilliant in the black velvet sky; somewhere an owl called, soft and low, and the bright copper shape of a fox trotted warily through the snow, leaving deep tracks in the sparkling white drifts.

Grandfather had loved snow. He would have loved the country. Why didn't he come to stay with them? Then they could all have been together for his last two years. A fresh tear rolled down Alice's cheek, chilling in the cold night air.

She imagined Grandfather's body lying in the cold earth, and an appalling memory gripped her. She remembered the day that Grandfather had taken her to her parents' funeral. Betty and Hester had stayed with Charlie's parents, but Alice had been old enough to wear a tiny black dress and go to the little church. Then, for the first time, Grandfather led her around to the cemetery behind the church.

They'd been walking toward the two neat graves dug for Mama and Papa when Alice had smelled something utterly vile. Something rotten and disgusting. It had made her gag, and Grandfather had pulled out his handkerchief and put it over her mouth and nose.

"What is that, Grandpapa?" she'd whispered.

Grandfather had been honest. "It's a pauper's grave, my poppet."

"What's that?"

"A place where poor people are buried."

Alice hadn't seen the pauper's grave, but she would never forget that smell. She leaned her head against the cool glass of the window, knowing that she'd be blamed when the curtains were opened, and the mark was discovered.

"Oh, Grandpapa," she whispered. "What did they do to you? Where are you?"

Had they thrown him into the stinking pauper's grave? Did his treasured bones lie there, picked at by crows? The thought made nausea rise in her belly, and Alice swallowed it down with an effort.

If only Grandfather could have been buried out here, under the clean crisp air. Perhaps under the great old oak that spread its branches so splendidly in the corner of the meadow. In winter he would slumber beneath a blanket of snow, the stars brilliant between the gnarled tangle of the oak's branches. In the summer he would be covered by a waving mass of knee-deep green hay, richly fragrant, peppered with wildflowers and field mice and tiny birds that perched on bending stalks of grass.

But none of that was Grandfather's reality. He was dead, and his bones rotted in a pauper's grave.

Alice pressed a fist against the window, biting back more tears. No. Surely, surely someone would have made sure that Grandfather was given a proper burial in a grave with a pretty headstone, right beside Mama and Papa… But Alice didn't know.

The only person who would know was Charlie.

Biting back sobs, Alice sank to the ground, rested her arms on the windowsill, and cradled her aching head in them. It had been so long since she'd allowed herself to think of Charlie and his kind spirit and his gentle eyes.

"Oh, Charlie, Charlie," she whispered, the words torn up by sobs. If she could only talk with Charlie, he'd tell her everything; what had happened to Grandfather, where he was buried, if he had suffered... if he had still loved her and her sisters to his final breath.

More than anything, Charlie would understand her in a way that no one had understood her since she'd left London. At the very least, he would care. Her heart screamed to see him. To see anyone who would look at her with kindness.

She wanted to get to London. No—she *needed* to get to London and find her answers. But how?

Alice opened her burning eyes and gazed across the snowy meadow, and like an answer to her question, the gleaming steam train chuffed across the landscape, scattering winter birds as it sped along the rails. It had to go to London, didn't it? Everything went to London eventually.

Sometimes, it even stopped near the village, for goods or passengers.

Alice watched the train go by underneath the stars, and her plan took shape.

TOMORROW WAS CHRISTMAS DAY, and Alice knew that she had no choice but to make this work tonight or she would never be able to find her answers.

It was the third night that she'd been sneaking down to the spot where the train stopped. It was not so much a train station as a lonely platform at the edge of the village, wrapped in snow, where farmers could occasionally load up their goods. But for the previous two nights, the train had not slowed down. It had simply chuffed on past, taking its bright light and its cheery noise and all of Alice's hope with it.

She thought Eleanor had been looking at her strangely at supper tonight. If Eleanor suspected her... if she was caught... It was unthinkable. Alice was already taking a risk sneaking out tonight. She knew that Mary would be furious when she returned in the morning either way, but then at least she would know. The worst thing that could happen would be if someone caught her before she got to London.

And that meant that she had to get on this train tonight.

She huddled by the wooden platform, trying to get out of the piercing wind that shrieked between the wooden struts and pressed its cold claws against her neck where her scarf didn't quite meet her hat. In the distance, she heard it coming, the chuff-chuff-chuff of the pistons, and a light glimmered on the dark horizon.

Alice braced herself. The moment that train stopped, she would run for dear life and scramble on board, and then she would hope with all of her heart that it would stop somewhere near the docks. Briefly, she remembered the stinking man who had tried to grab her and her sisters all those years ago. She pushed the thought away. She would fight twenty of those men if it would get her to Charlie.

The train came nearer; the ground quaked as it approached. Alice held her breath and squeezed her eyes shut, and for the first time in a long, long time, she prayed. *Oh, God, please let it stop. Please let it stop.*

Then she heard it: the screech of brakes.

Her eyes snapped open. The train was stopping. She could see the sparks flying from the tracks as it slowed. Leaping to her feet, Alice tensed, every muscle in her body tight as her heart hammered in her chest.

The great engine sped past her, and for a moment she thought it would vanish into the dark as it had done both nights before. But it didn't. Three cars rushed past—passenger cars—and then there were the ugly wooden cars that carried the cargo, and then it stopped, and a cargo car was right in front of her.

A head popped out of the train's window. "Hurry up." the conductor yelled.

Alice froze, terrified that he was talking to her, but then one of the passenger cars opened and someone jumped to the ground, shouting thanks. And the train once again began to move.

"No," Alice yelped.

She rushed forward, heedless of who might see her, eyes fixed on the open doorway of the nearest cargo car. The wheels and pistons moaned as the train began to move forward. Alice changed her course, sprinting through the snow that blew up in white powder around her knees, and reached the car a split second too late. The door was ten feet to her left and beginning to gain speed.

Charlie. The thought of his blue eyes spurred her on, and as the whistle shrieked, Alice drove her tired legs faster. Her fingers found the edge of the door, and she hauled herself up, kicking her legs in terror to avoid the spinning wheels. Her foot found purchase on something—she didn't have time to look and see what it was—and with a great effort, she hauled herself onto the dusty, smelly floor of the car.

She lay there for a few seconds, panting, feeling the soft rocking of the train as it sped onward through the dark night. The floor was sticky; her palms and cheek felt horrid where they pressed against it, but still, she was limp with relief. She'd made it.

"Oi," a gravelly voice snarled. "What's all this, then?"

Terror lanced through Alice's limbs. She scrambled backwards and pinned herself into a corner between some wooden boxes.

Had some train worker found her? Would he toss her out into the snow at this speed and break all her bones? Or would he simply dump her off at the next stop, miles from home, with no way of knowing where she should go or how to get there?

But the figures on the other side of the car didn't look like employees. Instead of uniforms, they wore tatty rags. Their bodies were no bigger than Alice, but their gnarled faces were shockingly adult; one had the first straggles of a beard. Their dark eyes glittered as they stared at her.

They were stowaways like her, Alice realized, but the knot in her gut only tightened. The desperation in their eyes reminded her of the old hag.

"What do you want?" the bearded one demanded. He clutched a long stick that had been sharpened to a point.

"Nothing," Alice cried, raising her hands.

"Why did you get onto our train, then?" the clean-shaven one snapped.

Alice swallowed. "I just want to go to London, to the docks. That's all."

"A likely story," the clean-shaven one hissed. "You got on this train because you're after something."

"You can't have our money," snapped the bearded one.

"I don't want your money," said Alice. "I just want to go to London."

The bearded one brandished the stick, and Alice screamed and cringed back against the boxes, trembling.

"Well, you might not *want* anything of ours," said the clean-shaven one slowly, "but maybe that's because you have money of your own."

The bearded one's eyes gleamed, and the clean-shaven one rose to a crouch.

"I don't," Alice cried. "I don't have anything. Look." She turned out the pockets of her dress and apron and spread her shaking, sweaty hands.

The clean-shaven one sat down again. "Well, all right. But don't come any closer.

The bearded one waved the stick.

Alice wedged herself tightly into the corner by the boxes. "I won't," she whispered.

※

ALICE'S LEGS ached from the way she crouched, but she dared not move them.

The two older boys had fallen asleep, but the bearded one still had the stick in one hand. When they slowed at a small village that Alice didn't recognize, he jumped up and waved the stick with a snarl, making Alice scream and press herself tighter into her corner. He had stared around with wild eyes, then snarled at Alice, jabbed the stick in her direction, and settled down again. Ever since, Alice had been too afraid to move.

The cold was ferocious. The wind blew in through the open car door, bringing fistfuls of snowflakes with it. Every house they passed had golden light coming from the windows, which only made Alice feel even colder. She shivered, arms wrapped around her body, watching as a grey dawn broke. It was Christmas Day, then. She had never been so cold before.

She was trying to keep herself from nodding off when she smelled it: a change in the air, something crisp and salty, mingled with pollution and tar. The smell was foul in its way, but it made her heart leap with hope.

They were nearing the docks.

The train's whistle shrieked, and the door was briefly draped in a white cloud of stream. Then they were over the hill and rushing down toward the great black smear of London, smog hanging low over its rooftops, the lazy Thames winding sluggishly through its heart. Alice almost laughed; she bit back the sound just in time. The boys sat staring, dull and uninterested.

When they rolled to a halt at a bustling train station, everything was covered in ribbons and wreaths, and there was a huge Christmas tree inside the building. Alice stirred, but the boys drew back further, vanishing into the gloom. They must be going somewhere other than London, she supposed. For her, this was the closest the train would bring her to the docks, at her best guess. She'd have to find her way to Grandpapa's cottage from there.

It would be empty, she knew. Boarded up perhaps or occupied by others. But it would still be there. Maybe it would smell like him.

She stumbled to her feet, then fell to her knees, clumsy with the ache in her muscles. Wincing, Alice drew her feet under her again and hopped down from the car.

She realized her mistake instantly. This was no snowy wasteland of countryside; this was a bustling station, and a small army of men in cloth caps and scarves were already making their way toward the car.

"Oi," one of them yelled. "Was she in the car?"

Alice froze.

"She must be a thief." another cried. "Get her."

They charged, and Alice spun and ran for her life. This part of the station was chaotic. Cargo lay everywhere, barrels and boxes, beams and livestock in pens, milling and lowing. There were people swarming on the tracks, even on Christmas Day. Alice didn't think; there wasn't time. She just bolted, ducking and dodging, weaving through the chaos, changing directions every time someone stepped into her path.

Her legs protested at being pushed to their fullest effort, and the cold air stung all the way down into her lungs, but scorching terror forced her to run faster. She vaulted over a fence and found herself in a pen full of sheep; they scattered, bleating in terror, and Alice pawed her way through the mass of woolly bodies, reached the other side and hauled herself over the wall. It was higher than she'd expected, and she landed awkwardly, feeling something crunch in her ankle, but she was free. A street stretched out before her, and her pursuers' voices were lost amid the bleating of the sheep.

Alice didn't look back. She bolted down the street as fast as her throbbing ankle would carry her, dived down an alleyway, and kept running, always heading for the smell of the sea.

CHAPTER 9

THE DOCKS WERE SO MUCH BIGGER than Alice remembered.

She'd thought it would be simple. She would find the docks, follow them to the cottage she'd loved, and then go to Charlie's home and see him. He would be there, of course. It was Christmas Day, after all. Where else would he be? Unless he had moved away, or been sent to the workhouse, or gone out to sea, or died...

No. Alice hugged herself tightly against the freezing wind that pressed handfuls of snowflakes into her face. Charlie couldn't be dead, because if he was, then all her hope had died with him.

She plodded along the docks beneath the towering masts of the ships that lay at anchor in the frigid water. There was hardly anyone here, but every home and tavern near the docks burst with light, music and delicious smells. More than once, Alice caught a whiff of glorious roast goose.

Though it was cold and pointless, the sun was high in the sky. Maybe everyone was sitting down to Christmas lunch already; Betty and Hester, Eleanor and Mary and Roger. Did they miss her? Had her little sisters even noticed that she was gone?

Alice was consumed by these gloomy thoughts when she spotted it: the dock where Grandfather's fish stand used to be. There was still a little stand there, right on the end, but Alice couldn't bring herself to look at it. The thought of that stand empty and alone was enough to press a dagger into her belly. At least it meant that she knew where she was now, and her pace quickened as she hurried toward Charlie's house.

The memories pursued her everywhere, like insistent ghosts. She passed the broken barrels and remembered Hester's screams when the old hag grabbed her. She passed the footpath leading to the beach where they'd found their driftwood Christmas tree, and she remembered Grandfather's laughter.

Tears rolled down her cheeks, but the sight of Charlie's cottage made Alice brush them away. Her heart lifted. The cottage was smaller and scruffier than she remembered, with grimy walls and cracked windows, but the wisp of smoke rising from the chimney was real and fragrant, and so was the green wreath hanging on the door.

Alice's heart thundered. She quickened her step, almost running to the door, and knocked.

"Coming," boomed a voice that was deeper than Alice remembered. Her heart skipped a beat. Could she be wrong? Did another family live here now?

The door swung open, and all her doubts cleared like mist in sunshine. It was Charlie, her Charlie. He was two years older now, with broadened shoulders and the rolling voice of a man, even a few hairs clinging to his upper lip. But nothing could ever change those blue eyes or the smile that lit him up like a lighthouse.

"Alice?" he rumbled.

"Charlie." Tears started down Alice's cheeks. "Oh, it's you. It's really you."

"What are you doing here?" Charlie asked.

"I came to see you." Alice froze. "Is... is that all right?"

"All right?" Charlie laughed; she'd forgotten how low and down-to-earth the sound really was, steady as a strong foundation. "Oh, Alice, it's wonderful, truly wonderful."

He held out his arms, and Alice didn't care if it was proper or not. She rushed into them, and he hugged her, smelling of the sea. She buried her face in his coat and hugged him back, sobbing with joy. It was the first time in two years that anyone had been truly glad to see her except for dear old Mrs. Porter.

"You've grown so much." Alice stepped back.

Charlie laughed. "So have you. It's been so long. Two whole years, to the day."

"I knew you'd remember," said Alice. "I knew you'd be glad to see me."

"Glad to see you?" Charlie smiled. "I've never been so happy in my life. When did you get here?"

"Just now. I, um... I took a train." Alice brushed away her tears. "I know that Mary will be furious—probably already *is* furious. I can only hope that she'll take me back. But I don't care. I just had to come and see you."

"Oh, Alice." Charlie gazed at her like the whole world turned around her. "I can't believe it's been so long. It's so good to see you again. How is the country? How have you been?"

"I've been missing you all," said Alice.

"Of course." Charlie lowered his head.

"The country is nice, I suppose. But I like it here much better," said Alice.

"Well, I don't know about that, but I'm glad to see you," said Charlie.

Alice lowered her head. "Do you mind if I ask you something?"

"Not at all. What is it?"

Alice took a deep breath. "Charlie... do you know..." She struggled against the lump in her throat. "How did my Grandpapa die?"

Charlie stared at her.

"I'm sorry to ask you," said Alice. "I know it's horrible. It's just..." The tears overwhelmed her, and she couldn't speak.

"Oh no, Allie, it's not that," said Charlie. "I'm surprised you're asking me because, well... Mr. Pryor isn't dead."

Alice's world stopped. "What?"

"Who told you that he was dead?" Charlie asked.

A sad suspicion and a wild hope grew together in Alice's heart. "Mrs. Hardin did."

"Well, he's not," said Charlie, "or at least he wasn't this morning, when we said merry Christmas to him at church."

Alice's heart was thudding so hard that she feared it would break clean through her ribs. She pressed her hands against it to stop it from escaping. "Grandpapa's alive?"

"Alive and well," said Charlie. "He misses you, but he's fine."

Alice pressed her cold hands against her cheeks. Was this real? Was this a wild dream?

"Come on." Charlie grabbed his coat from behind the door. "I'll take you to him."

He shrugged into the coat, whose sleeves were two inches too short and covered in patches, then reached out and wrapped his hand around Alice's. His fingers were very hard, but also very warm, and he held her hand gently as they headed down the street.

The whole world seemed suddenly far more beautiful to Alice as they walked. Charlie's was the only house with a wreath on the door, but everything else still shone with beauty; the grey sky, the distant sun, even the grey sea that rolled sluggishly to a windswept beach. It was suddenly the most wonderful Christmas of Alice's life.

"Grandpapa's alive?" she said. "He still has his fish stand?"

"Oh, yes. He's the same as ever," said Charlie. "Just sadder, I suppose, since he sent you all away."

Alice shook her head. "Well, now I know that he's alive, I won't ever have to go away again. I can stay here with him and with you." She sighed with relief. "Betty and Hester are happy where they are, but now everything can go back to the way it used to be."

"I don't know," said Charlie.

Alice stared at him. "Why not?"

"Well... things have changed here, Allie. Not your grandpapa. I don't think he *can* change." He laughed a little. "But this place... it's different. More and more of the bad sorts from the city have come to live here. They've built a new tenement just behind our street, and there are so many thieves and crooks and—and—ah—ladies of ill repute—" His ears glowed red.

"Oh," said Alice.

"You don't *want* to live here anymore," said Charlie. "Not if you can live in the country."

"Oh, Charlie." Alice squeezed his hand. "You don't understand the way the people are there. Not everyone." She thought of Mrs. Porter. "But I'd far rather stay here, no matter how many thieves or tenements or scoundrels there are."

"I suppose," said Charlie reluctantly.

There was a pause before Alice said, "I've missed you."

Charlie's fingers tightened on hers. "I've missed you, too."

Alice supposed she was too young to know what love was, but she felt then that she loved Charlie in a way she had never loved anyone.

"We're here," he said.

She raised her head, and there it was, straight ahead. Grandfather's cottage. *Her* home. Her heart flipped over and over in her chest, especially when she saw the poor bare front door with no decorations, and the windows without any mistletoe, and then, through the kitchen window, the big man sitting at the kitchen table all alone. He was spooning up mouthfuls from a little bowl; the contents looked grey, like porridge.

"Grandpapa," she croaked.

Charlie stopped. "I'll leave you to see him," he said, "but I do hope I'll get to see you again later, Allie."

Alice beamed up at him. "You will. You will. And oh, Charlie—thank you." She gave him a last hug, then pulled away from him and ran across the street to the front door.

Her hand was shaking so much that she could barely knock. She heard the familiar old creak of Grandfather's chair being pushed back—oh, how she'd missed the simplest of sounds—and the steady tread of his boots. Then he swung the door open and stood over her, broad-shouldered, bearded, his hair messy on his shoulders, his eyes the colour of the ocean, smelling as always of fish and salt and the open sky.

Grandfather's face froze. Tears suddenly filled his eyes, but his mouth did not move.

"Grandpapa," said Alice.

Her grandfather crumpled. His face turned into a reddened mass of wrinkles, and he said nothing, but reached out and pulled her into his powerful arms and held her against him.

"Allie," he sobbed at length. "Oh, Allie."

Alice clung to him, to this pillar that held up her world. She had never felt anything so sturdy or immovable in her arms, and she relished it. They held each other for a few long, long moments, both weeping. Alice had never seen Grandfather cry of happiness before, but she knew it now.

"Come inside, my poppet," said Grandfather. "Come inside before you catch your death. Where are Mary and the others?"

Alice hastened into the cottage, which was just the same as she'd left it, although perhaps a little dirtier and a little more run-down. "They're still in Edgeword, Grandpapa."

Grandfather's face stilled again. "Ah," he said. "I... I see." He paused. "Would you like some tea?"

"I'll make the tea," said Alice.

Being back in her kitchen was like being home. She still knew exactly where to fill the kettle and where to find the tea, and in a few moments, she had poured and strained it and given Grandfather a cup exactly the way he liked it. She hadn't had tea with milk in it for so very long, but now she added a splash for herself, too, and nobody shouted at her, and nobody ridiculed her.

Instead, when she sat across the table from Grandfather, he gave her a long, long look and sipped his tea very slowly. Then his smile blossomed over his face, and he said, "Tell me how you are, my poppet."

Alice told him everything: about the way Mary and Eleanor were with her, about Mrs. Porter who was the only kind soul in her life, about Roger who had never wanted her and her sisters who seemed to have forgotten that she existed.

"I don't think I blame them for it, Grandpapa," she said, "because they're very little, but it still hurts my heart so much."

"I see," said Grandfather. "I see." He took another long sip of his tea, which had long since grown cold.

Alice leaned forward. "But it's all right now, isn't it? I can stay with you now... can't I?"

Grandfather was silent for a long second. He stared into his mug, and Alice's heart dropped through the pit of her stomach.

"Grandpapa?"

"I'm so sorry, my poppet." Grandfather's shoulders sagged. "You can't stay."

Tears filled Alice's eyes. "I'll do anything," she begged. "I'll work for you. I'll make this house perfect again. I'll get a job. I'll—"

"It's not about you, my love." Grandfather reached across the table and engulfed her tiny hand in his huge one. "Perhaps you didn't understand this when I first sent you to live with Mary, but now you're old enough and you'll know. This neighbourhood simply isn't safe for you anymore. Perhaps it never was." He shook his head and shivered. "The things that happen to lovely, pretty girls like you in this place... They don't bear speaking about."

"I can take care of myself," Alice whispered, tears rolling down her cheeks. How could she be torn so brutally from her grandfather's arms all over again?

"I know you can, but there are evils in this world that are too strong for you," said Grandfather. "I can't put that responsibility on you, Allie. You shouldn't have to keep yourself safe; you should be safe where you are. The only place I can make sure of that is with Mary and Roger."

"But Grandpapa, it's awful there," Alice cried.

"Has anyone ever harmed you with their body?" Grandfather said, his voice suddenly sharp. "Has anyone ever physically hurt you in Edgeword?"

Alice was brought up short. She'd thought Mary might cuff her around the ears once or twice, but Grandfather was right. She was older now; she understood what he meant. She knew that there was not a mark on her body from physical harm.

"No," she admitted finally.

Grandfather sighed. "There's not a girl your age in this street to whom something hateful hasn't happened. I'm sorry, my poppet. You have to go back."

Alice hung her head, tears overwhelming her.

"I have missed you with all of my heart," said Grandfather, "but nothing is worth seeing you hurt."

"Grandpapa, please," Alice whispered.

"No, poppet. You're going back home, and that's final." Grandfather got up and pulled his coat close around him, "Cut yourself some bread and cheese for the journey, and then we'll go."

"Now?" Alice cried. "Can't I even stay for Christmas?"

Grandfather's face wobbled, and for an awful moment Alice was sure he would cry. Then he composed himself and said, "No. There is one last train to Edgeword leaving soon, and it'll be your only chance to get home before dark."

"But this is home," Alice whispered.

Grandfather looked at her, and the heartache in his eyes was so much worse than her own. Bad enough that Alice rose meekly and went to the cupboard to take out the same dear old breadboard and the same dear old breadknife and do as her grandfather said.

CHAPTER 10

Saying goodbye to Grandfather for the second time was infinitesimally worse than the first. Somehow, it felt as though Alice's entire body was being ripped in half when he pried her arms off him and said, "Go on, catch your train," with the tears glistening on his cheeks. She turned and scrambled onto the train, where she was crammed with the other third-class passengers like cattle. She wedged herself between an old woman and a pregnant girl and sat there staring after Grandfather, who waved and waved until the train was gone. The loss of it made her weep so despairingly that she didn't notice when the pregnant girl stole her bread and cheese from her bag.

It was only when the train stopped in Edgeword and Alice began the long dark trudge up the street toward the farmhouse that she realized how very hungry she was. She hadn't had a thing all day except for that one mug of wonderful tea. The memory of sitting across from her grandfather, pouring out her heart to him, while she sipped that delicious tea was enough to start the tears anew.

She dried them unsuccessfully by the time she reached the farmhouse and let herself quietly in through the back door. Perhaps if she slipped upstairs to bed, nobody would scream at her, at least, not tonight.

Alice was not so lucky. As she tried to tiptoe past the drawing room, a floorboard squeaked, and someone shouted, "Who's there?"

It was Roger, and his yell was loud and wobbly with eggnog. Dread built in Alice's belly. She dragged herself to the door of the drawing room and flung it open.

The Christmas tree glowed in a corner of the room. Betty and Hester sat near it, brown paper strewn around them, clutching new dolls and sweetmeats and oranges. Eleanor was in a back corner, arms folded and moody in her brand-new dress. Mary crouched by the little girls, and Roger sagged in his armchair, clutching a bottle, his mouth weighed down at the corners by drink.

"It's me," said Alice.

Mary raised her head. Her baleful grey eyes were as cold as slush.

"What are you doing here?" she hissed.

Alice swallowed. "I—I'm home."

"Home? Home? Why would you call this your home when you've run away?" Roger sprang to his feet with startling speed. "You left the roof I've put over your head and the food I've put in your plate to do what—to gallivant with some *boy*?"

"What? No," Alice cried. "I would never."

"You ungrateful wretch!" Roger roared and struck her.

The blow landed on her cheekbone and made her stumble backward. Alice gasped, clutching her injured face, and stared at him with tears rolling down her cheeks.

Mary was right behind him. "How dare you disrespect all that we have done for you," she spat. "Where did you go? What were you thinking?"

"I went to see Grandfather," Alice burst out.

Betty and Hester raised their heads. Mary turned a terrible shade of putty grey. "Come *here*," she snarled, grabbed Alice's arm, and dragged her into the hallway.

Alice's cheek ached where Roger had struck her. Her heart hammered as Mary cornered her in the hallway. "I told you he was dead," she hissed.

"You lied to me," Alice sobbed. "He's alive and safe, but he made me come back here."

"Well, that was his last mistake," Mary snarled. "I'll be rid of you yet, you little minx. You mark my words; I'll be rid of you. Now go to your room."

"But—"

"*Go!*" Mary yelled.

Alice saw danger in her eyes and felt the growing swelling on her cheekbone where she'd been struck. Tears flowing, she turned and bolted up the stairs to her room, sobbing with all her heart.

***

Eaton Country Estate was much less nice than it sounded.

Alice sat very quietly in the stagecoach, afraid to move beyond gazing out of the window. The landscape here was nothing like the softly rolling hills of Edgeword. Instead, a barren moor spread from horizon to horizon. There were no tilled fields and apple orchards; here the moorland was dotted with sheep, cows, pigs and ponies, and the woods were wild and gnarled.

She knew the great grey house the moment she saw it. It was a massive block of a building, with rows of symmetrical narrow windows that sneered out at the grey day. A bleak wind howled over the moors, banking snow against the stone walls and stripping the vegetation bare of anything but frost. It was colder than Alice had ever felt.

She shuddered as the stagecoach slowed near the back of the house and stopped.

"Get out," Mary barked.

Mary had been speaking in monosyllables ever since Alice had returned from London, and Alice had no idea why they were here; she only knew the name of this place because of the letters carved into a stone wall they'd passed earlier. Mrs. Porter had taught her that much, at least.

She wondered if this was a workhouse. She wondered if she would ever see Mrs. Porter again. At least she had gotten to see Grandfather one last time.

"I said, get *out*," snapped Mary.

Alice scrambled from the stagecoach. The wind snatched at her breath, and she wrapped her arms around herself.

"Get your bag," Mary ordered, stepping out.

Alice grabbed it. It was little more than a canvas sack, containing little more than a change of underwear. She clung to it as Mary strode away without another word; the stagecoach drove off, and Alice jogged after Mary.

The thin pathway to the estate's back door was overgrown with weeds and tussocks of grass that had frozen solid, catching Alice's toes. She was grateful for the excuse not to look at the vast house. With its stern pillars and narrow windows, it looked like it was sneering down at her.

Mary stopped when they reached the back door. She knocked once, and the door swung open, revealing a hefty woman whose apron was smeared with blood. She held a dripping cleaver, and her eyes were black and cold.

"What?" she snapped.

"Mrs. Cora Macready?" Mary asked.

The woman's eyes narrowed. "Yes."

"You wanted a scullery-maid. I saw your posting in the paper." Mary shoved Alice forward. "I've brought you one."

Mrs. Macready looked Alice up and down. "Bit old for a scullery-maid."

"Well, she's useless at everything, I'm afraid," said Mary. "Took this long just to teach her to scrub floors and wash dishes."

Alice stared at Mary, the untruth cutting deep into her soul.

"Why'd I want her, then?" Mrs. Macready snapped.

"Because you're shorthanded, aren't you?" said Mary. "I've worked as a cook, too. I know that this is the worst time of year to be without an extra pair of hands. Do you want her or not?"

Alice looked from one woman to the next, shocked that they were bargaining over her life as though she wasn't there. Her heart thudded. A scullery-maid? At least this place wasn't a workhouse, she supposed.

"Well, all right," said Mrs. Macready. "Can you polish silver, girl?"

Alice had to clear her throat twice before she could speak. "Yes, ma'am."

"Then get inside," Mrs. Macready snapped.

"Good." Mary turned away, and without saying a word of goodbye, she left.

PART III

CHAPTER 11

Three Years Later

The dull pain still throbbed in Alice's chest as she breathed the cold air of the scullery. She focused on taking slow, even breaths, her hands plunged in filthy, lukewarm water as she scrubbed the fine china on which the family had eaten their supper. Stuffed peacock with quail's eggs tonight. Alice wondered if she'd be lucky enough to get any meat at all.

A cough built in her chest, and Alice tried to stifle it, clearing her throat as she slipped the plate into the rinse water and reached for another. Her hands were careful, guarding the fine edges of each dish. She'd learned the hard way that chipping a dish had dire consequences in this house.

The cough continued to build despite her best efforts. Alice set the dish carefully in the rinse water, gripped the edge of the sink and spluttered, trying to hold it back, but the coughs escaped in a series of horrible, ripping heaves. Her lungs burned, and her eyes watered as she coughed.

The scullery door opened, and Mrs. Macready loomed in the doorway, her eyes narrowed. "What's wrong with you, child?" she barked. "It's been two weeks. How can you still be so ill?"

"I'm all right, ma'am," Alice croaked, wiping her mouth on her sleeve.

"You're spreading sickness wherever you go. Make sure you don't make the master's family sick, or there'll be consequences," Mrs. Macready snapped.

"I won't, ma'am," said Alice, not sure how she was meant to achieve this.

"Good." Mrs. Macready folded her arms. "When you're done with the dishes, fetch your things from your room. Then meet me in the hallway." She turned and strode away.

Alice's fear twisted in the pit of her belly, and she turned back to the dishes, trying to ignore her thudding heart. Was she about to be dismissed? And if she was, what would she do? It was the depth of winter; the moor was grey and covered with frost, and the wind hurled vengeful fistfuls of snow against the walls. She knew no one here. She had not left the grounds of the estate in three years.

Tears swarmed her eyes. A week ago, she had feared she would die. Now she feared she had survived her illness only to freeze on the open moor.

She plodded to the end of the dishes, dried the last one and put it up on the rack as the clock struck ten. In seven hours, she would be back down here again, lighting the fires... if she was lucky. Alice prayed silently that this would be the case. She wiped down the sink, hung the rags up to dry, and headed downstairs to the cellar to do as she was told.

Her room was in the bleakest, darkest part of the house, and hardly qualified to be called a room at all. The cellar was filled with sacks and sacks of coal. One corner had been cordoned off with some of those same coal sacks hanging on a string, and a tiny cot was pushed against the wall. The little trunk at its feet contained everything Alice owned.

She crouched down and opened it. It still held the same canvas bag with which she'd come here, with another black-and-white uniform and the few treasures she had gathered with her pitiful wages: a stub of pencil, a small and well-thumbed notebook, and a few stamps. Alice had hoped to write to Grandfather, but it was as though her ability to read had atrophied from lack of use. She had never been able to remember his address exactly, and by the time she thought she'd worked it out, she could hardly scribble a word anymore.

She gathered everything into the bag, scooped it up and stepped back to stare at her cot one more time. There was no sound of wind down here in the cellar; it felt like another world, and it was damp, and the air was thick with coal dust, which was what the doctor said—the doctor who had finally come when everyone, including Alice, was sure she would die—had caused her to get sick in the first place.

Now she was leaving. She had hated this place, but she had hated the moor far more.

There was nothing else for it. Alice turned and trudged out of the cellar, up the stairs and through the kitchen to the hallway.

Mrs. Macready was in the servants' hall, where everyone ate except for those who worked late, and spotted Alice through the open door. She rose to her feet and hurried up to her.

"What took you so long, child?" she growled.

"I was finishing the dishes, ma'am," said Alice.

"You cheeky wretch," Mrs. Macready sighed heavily. "If you weren't so hardworking, you'd be out on your ear just for the amount of lip you give me, do you know that?"

Alice stared at her. So she *wasn't* out on her ear?

"This way," Mrs. Macready ordered.

She strode up a narrow staircase at a speed that Alice found difficult to match. Her lungs were toiling by the time they reached the top of the house, somewhere near what had to be the attic; Alice couldn't tell, as she'd never been beyond the ground floor before. The hallway was bare and narrow, the walls whitewashed.

"Here." Mrs. Macready pushed open a narrow door. "Linny, Alice is going to stay with you, the way we talked about."

Alice peered into a tiny, dark room with a ceiling that slanted sharply. There was a single small window overlooking the snow-covered moor and, in each corner, a narrow bed. In between, there was hardly enough room to move.

The girl sitting on the bed on the left was so pale that she hardly seemed to have any pigment at all. Her skin was pale, her hair white blonde, her eyes so pale blue they were almost white. She smiled, her eyes vacant, as Alice came in.

"How lovely," she said, in a faint, fluttering voice.

"I'm going to stay here?" Alice whispered. The room was so much warmer than the cellar despite the wind that shrieked under the eaves just beyond the window.

"Yes. The doctor said it was the only way you'd live," said Mrs. Macready, "and I hope you're going to be grateful for it, child. You're lucky I even gave you a position in the first place with how poor your references were. Do you know how lucky you are to have all this?"

Alice looked around the tiny room and blinked back the tears of relief that filled her eyes. "I know, Mrs. Macready. Thank you."

FAYE GODWIN

Mrs. Macready slammed the door and strode away.

Alice clutched her bag to her chest and stared at Linny. The girl was a housemaid, one who swept floors and lit fires in the main house out of sight of the master and his family. They knew each other only vaguely.

"You can take that one," said Linny, pointing at the empty bed.

"Um—thank you." Alice sat down on it, holding her bag on her lap.

Linny swung her legs and smiled emptily. "It's nearly Christmas."

The word was like a punch to Alice's belly. It would be five years, this Christmas, since her world was turned upside down. She was fifteen; five years was nearly a lifetime. She stared at the floor.

"Don't you like Christmas?" Linny asked.

Alice raised her head, confused. The girl's smile was still in place. Was she... making conversation? She could hardly remember the last time someone had spoken civilly to her.

"I don't," she confessed. "I really don't."

"Oh, but why not?" said Linny. "The house is always so pretty, and there's always nicer food."

"That's true," said Alice. "I suppose bad things have just happened to me at Christmas, and now I don't like it anymore."

"I'm sorry," said Linny. "Bad things happened to me, too. I was in a workhouse before I came here. They beat me there. Sometimes they beat me here, too, but less." She giggled. "What happened to you?"

Alice couldn't stop herself. "My parents died."

"Mine too," said Linny. "They were brave sailors. Their ship sank and they drowned." She giggled. "That's what I tell myself, anyway. I don't really know what happened to them, but maybe they *were* brave. Maybe they were a doctor and a nurse, and they got the plague and died. Maybe they were farmers, and they died in a fire."

Alice understood. Maybe Linny's parents were anything except people who didn't want her and had left her on a workhouse doorstep.

"What about your parents?" Linny asked.

"They died in an accident," said Alice. "It was sad, but then I went to stay with my grandpapa." Her eyes filled with tears as sweet memories flooded her. "He lived in a cottage by the sea, and I stayed there with my two little sisters and him."

"Was he nice?"

"The nicest man you ever knew. He always spoke kindly to us and gave us everything we needed. We even played together sometimes." Alice swallowed against the tears. "Then it got too dangerous for me to stay there, so he sent us away to live with our great-aunt and great-uncle."

Linny let out a peal of laughter. "Oh, Alice, what an imagination you have."

"It was real," said Alice.

Linny smothered her laugh and nodded seriously. "Oh, I'm sure it was."

Alice sighed. Did it really matter if Linny believed her? Talking about Grandfather made him feel real again, no matter what Linny thought.

"There was someone else I cared about, too," she said. "Maybe even loved."

"*Loved?*" Linny leaned closer. "Was it a boy?"

Alice's cheeks flooded with heat. "Yes."

"Was he handsome?"

"Very handsome," Alice remembered. "He has the most marvelous blue eyes."

"Oooh." Linny tucked her hands under her chin. "What was his name?"

"Charlie. Charlie Tillman. He's very kind and gentle and loves little children."

"I think I should have a gentle beau with blue eyes, too," Linny giggled. "I'll name him... John."

Alice looked into her vacant eyes and couldn't help but smile. "John's a nice name."

"I think so, too." Linny threw herself onto her bed and sighed. "Maybe one Christmas we'll all have houses of our own. Me and John and you and Charlie. Maybe even babies."

Alice put down her bag and curled up on the bed, allowing herself to dream. "Maybe."

※

"ALICE, DID YOU SEE?" Linny hissed. "He's home."

Alice raised her head. It was a Sunday afternoon, their only time off for a rare few hours, and for once there was a little sunshine and no wind over the moor. She and Linny were taking the opportunity for a walk around the grounds, keeping to the vegetable garden and stable yard to avoid getting into trouble.

"Who's home?" Alice asked, nonplussed.

Linny's eyes sparkled. "George Eaton, of course."

It took Alice a few minutes to remember who that was. The youngest of the Eaton sons, he was usually away at boarding school.

"Oh," she said. "He must be on Christmas holidays now, I suppose. That means more work for you, doesn't it?" She thought of the extra plates and cups and knives and forks she would be washing that evening and stifled a sigh.

"What does it matter?" Linny giggled. "Look. There he is. Isn't he just *so* handsome?"

Hooves sounded on the road, and Alice jumped. A fine chestnut horse walked toward the stable yard, flanks streaked with sweat, surrounded by foxhounds. On his back, a young man held the reins loosely. He was only a year or two older than Alice and Linny, with a thin slice of moustache over his upper lip and a mop of dark hair.

"So handsome," Linny sighed.

The young man's eyes penetrated hers, and Alice looked away quickly. "I don't know. He seems... cruel."

"Nonsense," said Linny. "I think he looks lovely."

Alice felt his eyes on her as the chestnut horse came nearer. She prayed silently that he would ride into the stable yard and leave them alone, but instead, the horse's hooves clopped to a halt just across the fence from where Linny and Alice walked.

"Come on, Linny." Alice grabbed her elbow. "Let's get away from here."

"Don't be silly," said Linny.

"You there," George called.

Alice tried to hurry away.

Linny stopped. "Yes?"

"Not *you*," said George. "The pretty one."

Alice felt her cheeks burn. She stopped reluctantly.

George swung down from his horse and strode to the fence, resting his elbows on it. This close, he smelled of cigarette smoke, and his eyes were darker than ever.

"I've seen you before," he said. "You work in the kitchen."

"Yes, sir," said Alice nervously.

Linny let out a high-pitched giggle.

George barely spared her a glance; he was too busy looking at Alice, his gaze crawling up and down her body like spiders. "Why don't you meet me behind the stables in a few minutes, Alice?"

"To do what?" Linny asked.

George's expression left no doubts about that.

"Sir, I—" Alice began.

Hooves clattered deafeningly on the road, startling George's horse. The animal jumped back, yanking him several steps backward, as the master's proud black four-in-hand thundered down the road, drawing his large carriage.

"Come on, Linny." Alice grabbed her arm to hasten away.

"But Alice—" Linny began.

"Come *on*." Alice pulled hard, dragging Linny after her. By the time George had regained control of his horse, they were halfway across the garden already. Alice heard him shout something after her, and Linny slowed again, but she refused to let her stop until they were back in the safety of the kitchen.

"What did you do that for?" Linny demanded, pulling her arm out of Alice's grasp. "He was being so nice."

"We need to stay away from him, Linny," said Alice.

Linny stared at her, her eyes as empty as sunny summer skies. "But why?"

Alice swallowed, wondering how to explain. Perhaps she couldn't explain the horror in the pit of her stomach at the sight of George Eaton.

"Alice, you're being silly," Linny chided. "This is awfully romantic. Why, can't you see that George is madly in love with you?"

Alice shuddered. She didn't know much, but of this much she was certain: the look in George Eaton's eyes was by no means love.

※

THE KITCHEN WAS IN CHAOS. Maids and cooks bustled left and right, cowering under the barked orders from Mrs. Macready as savoury smells filled the air. Alice didn't know the names of half the dishes that bubbled on the stove or baked in the oven, but they all smelled incredible, making her belly grumble with hunger. It had been an awfully long time since the rusk and tea she'd had at ten o' clock between finishing the silver and starting on the floors.

She kept her head down, avoiding Mrs. Macready as she fetched and carried ingredients and equipment to the maids and cooks.

"Finer." Mrs. Macready bellowed at a hapless kitchen maid chopping onions. "Do you think you're making stew in some hovel? Chop those onions finer."

The maid was close to tears. "Yes, Mrs. Macready. Sorry, Mrs. Macready."

"Keep working," Mrs. Macready bellowed.

Linny burst into the kitchen, her eyes huge. "Oh, Mrs. Macready, it's a disaster." she wailed.

Alice cringed on Linny's behalf.

Mrs. Macready rounded on her. "What nonsense is this, child?"

"It's the big wreath in the dining hall. The leaves are all falling off," Linny cried. She held out a handful of dried holly leaves, browned and curling at the edges. "They're making a horrid mess on the floor, and the wreath looks *awful*. What are we to do?"

Mrs. Macready's ever-glowing face went a few shades redder. "We can't have that. The Parkinsons will be here in four hours. Whatever will they think if the wreath is falling apart?"

"The mistress will be furious," said Linny, and burst into tears.

Mrs. Macready squared her shoulders. "You'll have to go and get a new one."

"M–me?" Linny gasped.

"Does it look like anyone else has the time, child?" Mrs. Macready unlocked a box on the kitchen mantelpiece and took out some money. "Go straight to the village; there are plenty of hawkers selling Christmas wreaths at the market. Buy the nicest one you can find."

She thrust the money into Linny's hand, and the girl stared at her with huge, terrified eyes, her lower lip trembling. "Nicest? What does that mean? Biggest? Should it have holly berries?"

"Clearly you can't go alone," Mrs. Macready snapped. She whirled around. "You. Scullery-maid."

Alice froze.

"Yes, you. Go with Linny at once," said Mrs. Macready. "There's no time to waste. Get your coat and go."

Linny's face lit up.

Alice's heart flipped with sudden excitement. "Yes, Mrs. Macready." She seized her tattered coat from behind the kitchen door before the old woman could change her mind, and she and Linny hastened out of the back door and down the path through the back of the estate toward the village.

Linny giggled as they left the confines of the estate behind and started along the lane that led through the woods to the village. "Can you believe it, Allie? Me and you going to the village, at Christmastime." Her eyes shone.

Alice smiled. "It's been such a long time since I've gotten to see a market. Why, I only saw the village once, and that was when I came here."

"Poor Allie." said Linny. "But don't worry. We'll get to see it now, and it'll be all splendid, decorated and pretty."

Alice thought the woods themselves were splendid enough for now. It was snowing just lightly, a fine white dust that settled over the thick tangle of the trees like icing sugar, and their feet crunched quietly on the fine layer of snow that covered the lane. The cold made Alice's nose burn, but there was no wind. She tipped her chin and breathed the fresh air deeply, relishing the feeling of being outside, of seeing something new.

I think God does the prettiest Christmas decorations, Grandfather had told her one time as they gazed across the snow-dusted beach. Alice now knew what he meant.

Hoofbeats thudded behind them, and Alice grasped Linny's arm to steer her off the path and out of the way of the rider. But when she glanced over her shoulder, she saw a flash of chestnut, and her heart dropped abruptly into her boots, leaving a cold and empty space in her chest.

George reined in the horse a few feet from them and leaped carelessly from the animal's back. It snorted at him, plumes of steam from its nostrils, and hung back as he strode toward the girls.

Alice's first instinct was to run, but where could she go that the horse's swift hooves couldn't follow? The woods were not dense enough for her to slip away through the branches.

"Hello there," he called.

Linny all but melted. "Oh, hello, Master George."

George didn't look at her. "Where are you off to on such a cold day, you pretty thing?"

Alice recoiled. "We're going to the market. In fact, we need to get there right away." She tugged Linny's arm. "We're in a hurry."

Linny giggled. "Oh, Master George, we're going to get a new wreath for the dining room. Then it'll be beautiful for your guests."

"Guests." George scoffed. "What a bore. I'd far rather be out here with you." His predatory eyes remained fixed on Alice's. "What's your name?"

"We need to go," said Alice.

"Alice," said Linny. "And I'm Linny."

"It's nice to officially meet you, Alice." George's grin widened. "I've been trying to catch your name for a while now."

Alice's gut twisted. It had been a week since he'd approached her outside, and she'd been hoping that she'd imagined the times that he always seemed to be nearby the moment she set foot out of the kitchen, or the time he'd followed her as far as the landing to the servants' quarters before his father had called him back.

"Alice is afraid of you," Linny blurted. "Isn't she silly?"

George's eyes darkened. "Very silly. What on earth would there be to be afraid of?"

"That's what I said," said Linny. "You're just lovely."

Now, George finally looked at Linny, and his hungry gaze devoured her from head to foot. "You're quite right," he said, winking. "I *am* lovely."

Linny's giggle was high-pitched, and she smiled widely.

"Linny, we need to go." Alice pulled at her arm.

"What's the hurry, Allie?" Linny ripped her arm away. "George and I are talking."

"Yes, what are you in such a hurry for?" George asked. He wrapped an arm around Linny's shoulder. "We're having a good time here. I'm so lonely in that big, cold house. Don't be so mean."

Linny squeezed her body against George's, almost hysterical with giggles now. "How could you be mean, Alice?"

George reached for Alice's arm, but she retreated a few steps and planted her hands on her hips. "Don't touch me." she snapped. "I know what you're doing. Now let Linny go. We're leaving."

"Alice," Linny gasped.

George's arm curled over Linny's shoulders, his fingers draping carelessly over her chest. She simpered, her eyes on his.

"Perhaps you should go on ahead, Alice," he said, "if you're going to be so difficult." His arm tightened. "We'll catch up."

"What?" Alice snorted. "Absolutely not. I'm not leaving her alone with you."

"Alice, stop being so rude," Linny cried. "How could you act like this?"

"He wants to hurt you, Linny," said Alice bluntly. "He doesn't love you."

The hurt in Linny's eyes was a blow to Alice's gut. "How can you say that?"

"How *can* you say that, Alice?" George spat. "You're just being cruel because I don't think you're pretty. Not like I think Linny is pretty." He pulled her closer. "Not like I love Linny."

Linny's smile said that all her dreams had just come true.

Alice took a deep breath. "Linny, you have to listen to me."

"Just go away, Alice," said Linny. "You're not wanted."

Alice's heart stung, but that didn't matter now. All that mattered was getting Linny away from George. "You're not listening. He's going to hurt you. Now get away from him, and let's get to the market."

She stepped forward, but George reached out and slammed a hand into Alice's shoulder, knocking her backwards. She landed heavily in the snow, her heart thundering.

"I said, *go away*," George snarled. "Or shall I tell my father that you're a promiscuous little wench and that you should be sent away?"

Alice's heart stuttered. George's father would believe him, and that would be the end of the only home and employment Alice had.

"Please don't," she croaked. "But please, please don't hurt Linny."

"If you don't leave, I'll make sure neither of you work at Eaton ever again," George growled.

Alice glanced at Linny, but the girl was smitten, dumbstruck. There was no reasoning with her.

She fought back tears as she rose to her feet. "All right," she whispered. "All right. I'm going."

But she only went as far as it took for her to no longer be able to hear their voices. Then she tucked herself into the woods and slipped through the undergrowth, going from tree to tree, holding her breath on each dash between the trunks. In a few minutes, moving as quietly as she could, she could hear them again.

"Oh, George," Linny giggled. "That feels so nice."

"Wait until you feel *this*," George growled.

Linny gasped.

Alice's stomach turned, but she pushed on, ducking under the branches. Their voices were still on the path. In a few minutes, Alice spotted them between the trees. George's horse was gone; he must have turned it loose. Now, Linny stood with her back to a tree, George's body pressed insistently against hers, his hands roaming freely over her. His mouth was on her cheeks, then her neck.

Alice's body trembled. Surely Linny must see now that George's intentions were far from good, but the girl's giggles were as gormless as ever.

There was nothing else for it. Alice stepped onto the path and shouted with all of her might, praying that someone in the estate or the village would hear.

"Hey," she yelled. "Get your hands off her."

George whipped around. "*You.*"

"Alice!" Linny cried, her hair in disarray.

"You leave her alone." Alice bellowed.

She knew she'd made a mistake when the expression in George's eyes changed. Darkened. Like a gas lamp switching off, he went from hungry to furious in an instant. She scrambled back, trying to run, but he was already upon her, seizing her by the hair.

Alice screamed. George slammed her against a tree trunk with a force that made stars pop in front of her eyes.

"Shut up," he growled.

Alice whimpered.

"George?" Linny gasped. "What are you doing?"

"Just making sure we won't be interrupted again, my love," George sang in a voice filled with sweetness.

Linny hesitated. "But you're hurting her."

"Oh no, darling. Allie and I are just playing," George hissed, his breath hot on Alice's ear. Her skin crawled.

Linny hovered.

George pressed her against the tree, his loathsome body against hers. "I should have my way with you here and now," he whispered. "I should teach you a lesson you'd never forget."

This was exactly what Grandfather was afraid of, Alice realized, her heart hammering wildly in her ears. This was exactly what he wanted to save her from. No wonder he would do anything, even break both of their hearts, to keep her safe from this.

A buckle jingled, and George raised his belt in one hand. Alice's heart stopped dead.

"But I'm in a hurry," he purred, "luckily for you. I don't have time for both of you. So, you're just going to have to stay here and freeze to death."

He wrapped the belt around her arms and chest, pulling it so tight that she yelped, then buckled it behind the tree. When he stepped back, the front of his trousers gaped loathsomely over his tucked shirt, wide as his grin.

"Come on, Linny, darling," he sang. "Let's go."

He took her hand, but Linny hesitated. "What about Allie?" she asked. "Why is she crying?"

"Oh, Allie's just jealous that we're not taking her with us," said George.

"Why can't she come?" Linny asked.

"Don't go with him, Linny," Alice croaked. "I beg you. Don't do it." But a look from George silenced her.

"She can't come because we're going somewhere very special," George purred. "Somewhere just for you and me."

Linny stared at Alice for a moment longer. Then she melted into giggles again as George led her away.

CHAPTER 12

Alice didn't know how long she was tied to that tree, but it was long enough for her feet to go numb and for pins and needles to prickle her hands as she strained to get them behind her, trying to reach the buckle.

It was long enough for something awful to happen, and certainly long enough for Mrs. Macready to think that she and Linny had made off with the money.

The tears had long since stopped coming. Terror sharpened Alice's senses into nothing but the tension of the belt around her body and what she had to do to get out of it.

She reached around again, her arms straining, and her fingertips brushed the hard metal of the buckle but could go no further. Her hands fell to her sides again, shoulders aching, fingers numb. Alice hung her head and held back her sobs.

"Come on, Alice," she whispered. "Come on."

It was still long before dark, but already a deathly chill crept across the moor, damp, and clinging. If she didn't get back before dusk, would anyone come looking for her? Would George come back this way? Would he suddenly decide that he *did* have the time?

What had he done to Linny?

The thought sent a pang of terror through her. Alice let out a scream and threw herself against the belt with all of her strength, and she felt something shatter in the tree, a piece of bark, a twig, she didn't know, but there was a sudden laxity in the belt. Panting, she sagged against it, considering her options, and tested its tightness with her arms.

Maybe... just maybe. Alice sucked in a breath and lowered herself very slowly. The belt snagged on something, but it slid upward, over her arms, reaching her shoulders. It grew tight then, but Alice kept easing herself down and down, her knees screaming, her back scraped raw, and finally it popped over her shoulders. She seized it and yanked it over her head, and she was free.

She didn't hesitate. Despite the stiffness in her legs and the numbness of her cold feet, Alice ran down the lane in the direction George and Linny had gone.

"Linny," she yelled. "*Linny*."

They had gone deeper into the woods than she'd expected. Suddenly she was out from among the trees and standing at the edge of the village, blinking in surprise, the afternoon sun still high. How was it possible that no one had heard her screams?

Perhaps someone had heard Linny.

"Linny," Alice yelled.

"Stop that racket," snapped an old woman sweeping the front step of her cottage. "You're disturbing the peace."

Alice stared at her. "Please, ma'am. I'm looking for my friend. She's blonde... very pale. Have you seen her?"

The woman sneered. "You mean the latest prize of George Eaton? Yeah, she was here."

"Where did she go?" Alice cried.

"How am I supposed to know?" the woman snapped. "Or care? She'll cause a scandal for him yet. She or one of the others."

"Ma'am, please," Alice yelped. "She's—she's a little slow. She doesn't know what she's doing."

The woman scoffed. "Any woman knows."

"Please," Alice begged.

The woman shrugged. "That way." She jerked her head in the direction of the market.

Alice ran there as fast as her legs would take her, ignoring the angry yells from other villagers. The market was small, but at this time of year, bustling. A fat woman sold live geese in wire cages; a man sold great sides of ham, and there was the old widow who made the wreaths, displaying them proudly on her table.

Alice looked left and right, but she couldn't find George or Linny. Where could they have gone in a tiny village like this?

Her eye caught on the wreaths again, and she realized how hard she was shaking, how hard her heart was pounding. What was she going to do? If she didn't bring a wreath back to Mrs. Macready, she'd be furious. Furious enough to dismiss her and Linny both? Alice thought so.

She took a deep breath, trying to calm her hammering heart. It was horrible to think of, but whatever George was going to do to Linny, he would have done it by now. Alice couldn't stop it. The reality crushed her, but it was true. The best she could do now was to make sure that she and Linny would still have a home and a job to get back to.

She stumbled to the wreath lady, grateful that she'd had the presence of mind to take the money from Linny as they'd left the house and bought the biggest wreath she could find. It seemed a silly thing now, pointless in its reds and greens and bright ribbons. The lady wrapped it in some brown paper and tied it with a string, which Alice looped over her shoulder like a bag as she turned toward home. Would Linny find her own way? She didn't know, but if she didn't return with this wreath right now, neither of them would have a home to return to at all.

Her head hanging, Alice plodded back through the woods, keeping a sharp ear out for the sound of footsteps. If George approached her now, she'd run for her life; maybe she'd be able to outrun him.

But when the sound echoed between the trunks, it wasn't footsteps. It was sobbing, and the voice was appallingly familiar.

"Oh, no," Alice whispered. "Linny?"

The sobs only intensified in response to her cry, but she jogged toward it, pushing through the branches, heedless of the twigs that tore at her clothes and the brown paper.

She found Linny in a clearing, lying on her side in the snow, curled up around her belly, her tears almost freezing to her face. The girl's hair was mussed, her bonnet gone. Snow and mud had smeared her back, face, and hair.

"Linny." Alice cried. She hung the wreath on a branch and fell on her knees beside Linny. When she touched her shoulder, the girl screamed and cowered.

"It's all right, Linny. It's me," said Alice. "It's me."

"Allie?" Linny whispered. "What did he do? What did he do?"

She rolled over, and Alice saw the ghastly red stain on her skirt. Her heart plummeted.

"Why?" Linny whispered, holding up bloodstained hands.

"I don't know," said Alice truthfully. "Let's get you home."

She pulled Linny to her feet. The girl cried and doubled over, clutching her abdomen, but Alice dragged her arm over her shoulders, grabbed the wreath and staggered home.

<hr />

"Where have you girls been?" Mrs. Macready thundered.

Alice stood in the doorway, her muscles trembling with fatigue, clutching Linny's arm in one hand and the wreath in the other. Reaching the warmth of the kitchen felt like a triumph so great that Mrs. Macready's yelling was barely a scratch on the surface of her wounded consciousness.

"*Where*—" Mrs. Macready shouted, striding out from the back of the kitchen.

She stopped when her eyes landed on Linny, dripping wet, her skirt soaked with blood. The girl stood mute, head hanging, hair stringy.

Alice knew that it would be pointless to say anything about George. She would be dismissed at once for lying; Linny too, in all likelihood.

"She was attacked," she said simply.

Mrs. Macready's eyes said that she understood and that this was not the first time. Her lips drew down, and she shook her head.

"Oh, Linny," she said. "You always were a stupid girl."

"Here's the wreath," said Alice, holding it out.

Mrs. Macready took it.

"I don't think she can work," said Alice.

"Then you shall do both of your work." Mrs. Macready's lips pressed into a thin line. "Go to your room, Linny."

The girl dragged herself across the kitchen, and Alice watched her go.

"Go on," snapped Mrs. Macready. "You have double the work now, and the Parkinsons will be here in two hours."

Had they really been gone only two hours? It felt like an eternity, to Alice. But she quickly learned what an eternity truly felt like. An eternity was how long it took to finish all the preparations for the dinner, including Linny's work in the rooms. It was how long it took to wash all the dishes afterward, to scrub all the floors, to polish all of the silver, and to collapse, numb, aching and delirious, into bed after one in the morning.

ON CHRISTMAS EVE, Linny did not emerge from her room.

Alice tried to talk to her, but the girl lay on her side, curled under her covers, saying nothing. When Alice tried to touch her, she moaned and pulled away. There was no new blood that Alice could see; her cheeks were pink, and her skin was cool and dry. The girl's ailment wasn't merely physical, Alice knew.

"I'm sorry, Linny," she said. "Sometimes people do terrible things. It wasn't your fault. He's a monster."

Linny sobbed quietly into her pillow, and Alice left the room feeling like her heart was a lead ball far too heavy for her chest.

All that day, Alice scrubbed and polished, turned sheets and aired rooms, lit fires and threw away kitchen rubbish to the pigs, then washed dishes and washed and washed some more. She listened to the family laughing in the drawing-room and heard the happy squeals of people opening presents after dinner. She watched the roast goose go out with all its gorgeous golden trimmings, feeling the pangs of hunger in her belly; she was far too busy for breakfast or lunch.

By the time she climbed the narrow steps to her room, she supposed that it was Christmas Day. It must have been past midnight, she thought, though she was far too tired to listen for the bell of the grandfather clock down in the drawing-room. She just wanted to crawl into her bed and sleep.

She stumbled into the room, glanced at Linny, but there was no movement from the bed; she must be asleep. If she was resting, Alice didn't want to disturb her. She kicked off her shoes, hung up her dress and apron so that she would not be punished for having wrinkled clothes, and fell into bed. Sleep came instantly.

ALICE FELT that she had barely closed her eyes when the bell struck five, her waking hour, and her eyes snapped open. Terror had long since trained her to wake at exactly five o' clock every morning to escape the wrath of Mrs. Macready.

All of Alice ached. She pressed her face into the pillow, her eyes crusty with sleep. She'd learned that there was no worse day of the year than Christmas Day. Memories clustered around her like vengeful ghosts, ready to attack. And for a scullery-maid, there was no rest, no merriment, and no gifts. Only an endless pile of work as the family of the house feasted without a second thought for where their plates and cups and knives and forks went when the meal was done.

She sat up slowly, pulling a hand through her tangled hair, ignoring the agony that shot through her back and shoulders from her time spent tied to a tree by George Eaton.

George. *Linny.* Alice's head snapped around, and she fumbled for the matches next to her bed. She couldn't see to the other side of the room; it was utterly pitch dark. The candle next to

Linny's bed must have burned down and gone out in the night. She struck a match and lit her own candle, then held it aloft in a shaky hand.

"Linny?" she whispered.

There was no sound or movement from beneath the rumpled blankets.

Alice's heart stabbed sharply through her chest. She pushed back her covers, lowered her bare feet to the floor that was so cold it burned, and stumbled over to the bed. Had Linny died, and she didn't know? She'd been so tired last night. Oh, why hadn't she checked?

"Linny," she cried, grabbing the girl's shoulder.

But her fingers found no solid flesh. They sank through fabric, and she pulled back the covers to find that Linny wasn't in bed at all. The way the blankets lay had tricked her eyes in the dark.

Where was she?

There was only one explanation: hurt, confused, and scared, Linny had run away. Why would she not? She could barely understand what had happened to her, as if understanding would make it any less appalling.

Alice put down the candle, threw on her clothes and put up her hair as quickly as she could. She had to fumble in the covers for the bonnet she'd forgotten to remove last night.

Tying the straps under her chin, she ran out of the door and bounded down the stairs at a reckless pace, ignoring the thunder of her feet or the pangs in her knees and ankles.

She didn't know which room belonged to Mrs. Macready, but on a day like Christmas Day, it wouldn't be very long before the head cook was downstairs getting ready. Fear stung her hands and made them work quickly as Alice lit the kitchen fire, stoked the coal stove, and set out all the necessary pots and pans and utensils for breakfast. Her heart thudded uncomfortably in her throat. If it wasn't for her fear of dismissal by Mrs. Macready, she would already be out there, looking for Linny. What if she was lost in the snow?

Alice was setting out the breakfast dishes when Mrs. Macready finally came down to the kitchen, looking even more short-tempered than usual. She didn't care.

"Mrs. Macready," she cried.

The cook glared at her as she slammed a cast-iron pan down on the stove. "What is it, child?"

"It's Linny," said Alice. "She's gone. I don't know if she was in our room when I went up last night, but she's not there now. We have to go looking for her. She's hurt, and I don't know if she's in her right mind. She could be anywhere. She must have run away."

"Don't be so hysterical," Mrs. Macready snapped. "The girl didn't run away."

"But where could she be, then?" Alice cried.

"I hardly care. I told her that her best chance would be the workhouse in town," said Mrs. Macready, "especially if she turns out to be with child."

The thought hadn't even occurred to Alice. It took her a second to get past the shock of the possibility and reach the word *workhouse*.

"I... I beg your pardon?" Alice stared at the woman. "Why... why would you... isn't she here?"

"No," said Mrs. Macready. "She has been dismissed, stupid girl." She looked away. "Bring me the cleaver for this bacon."

"Dismissed." Alice's heart stuttered. "But she's hurt."

"What use do you think she would be to this household?" snapped Mrs. Macready. "The cleaver, *if* you please."

Alice couldn't move. She stared at the cook, wondering how many of the other maids that had come and gone in the last three years had fallen prey to the same fate as Linny. What of the maid that had vanished and left behind the position that Alice had filled, also at this time of year? Had she, too, been a victim of George Eaton, and then cast out into the cold and inhospitable winter like a discarded rag?

"Alice," Mrs. Macready snapped. "Bring me that clever."

The wind howled around the edges of the kitchen, but suddenly Alice could not bring herself to care.

"No," she said.

Mrs. Macready's eyes narrowed. "Choose your words carefully, girl."

"No," said Alice. "I won't be a part of this any longer."

Mrs. Macready's cheeks reddened to crimson.

"You know exactly what George does to us," said Alice. "You know what he did to Linny, and you know what he'll do to me if he has the chance, but you say nothing. You do nothing."

"There is nothing *to* do," said Mrs. Macready. "It's the way of the world."

"It shouldn't be, and it doesn't have to be. Your silence makes you complicit," said Alice, "but mine will not do the same to me."

"You will have no references," Mrs. Macready growled.

"At least I will not be you," said Alice.

Mrs. Macready's face crumpled, and for a second, tears filled her eyes. "Now look here—"

Alice had no interest in listening. She set down her broom with a light touch and turned to walk up the stairs. Her old, tattered dress, the one that really didn't fit anymore, was still at the bottom of her bag; she exchanged her uniform for those rags, took what little she owned, and walked back to the kitchen.

By now, the kitchen was filled with maids, and they followed her with a battery of glares as she strode to the door. She wondered briefly what Mrs. Macready had told them, then realized that she didn't care.

"You'll starve," Mrs. Macready growled. "You have nowhere to go, you stupid wretch, don't you know that?"

Alice turned with her hand on the doorknob and looked her in the eye. "I know that," she said. "Linny didn't. But you sent her away anyway. You're as much of a monster as he is."

She left then, closing the door quietly behind her, and walked out into the frigid morning, still dark, the cold merciless against her skin. She wondered for a moment if the shock in Mrs. Macready's face would be enough to change anything in this detestable place.

Maybe, maybe not. Alice supposed she'd never know.

CHAPTER 13

It was late evening, and the vibrant joy of Christmas morning had matured into quiet contentedness. At least, this was what Alice imagined was happening inside the cottages of Edgeword as she gazed through the window of the stagecoach as it rocked its way down the hill into the village. They were all lit up with golden firelight, the Christmas trees colourful in the windows, the wreaths dusted with a powdering of snow.

Alice pressed her hand into her apron pocket and felt the last few coins at the bottom. She had hardly spent any of her tiny wages earned at the estate, but even so, it had cost her almost everything she had to get to her destination.

The coach approached the little farmhouse at the edge of town, and Alice's belly tightened as she leaned nearer the window, trying to see inside.

"Here, miss?" said the driver.

Alice was alone for this part of her journey; they'd dropped the other passengers in a larger village nearby. She had no idea how she had been lucky enough to find a kindly driver who'd take a detour into Edgeword for a few extra pennies.

"Yes," she said. "Right here."

The stagecoach rumbled to a halt. Alice pressed herself against the window and looked into the drawing-room. The Christmas tree stood just where it had been three years ago, adorned with the same ribbons, but new gingerbread men. Roger sat in an armchair, his nose buried in a glass of eggnog.

The sight of Hester made tears fill Alice's eyes. She was ten now, the age Alice had been when she'd first come here, and she wore a new, pretty dress. She and Hester sat on the sofa, reading. *Reading.*

They didn't need her, Alice realized, as if she could have helped them even if they did, any more than she could help poor Linny, wherever she had gone. There was only one thing left for Alice now.

"Thank you," she said. "We can go."

"To London, miss?" the driver asked, raising an eyebrow.

Alice knew that look. She handed him her last few coins.

"To London," she said.

So much had changed in just three years.

It seemed impossible for these towering tenement buildings to have sprung up on this dear old street so quickly, but they had. There were almost no cottages left. As Alice stumbled up the street in semi-darkness, lit only by the new street lamps by the sides of the road, she kept her arms wrapped around herself against the icy wind that howled in over the sea. One giant, ugly, blockish building after the other greeted her where cottages used to be. Each building was three or even four stories, much taller than Alice was used to seeing, and each looked like it had been slapped together hastily with no regard for the people who would have to live there. The mortar was already crumbling between the bricks. Chinks of light escaped through holes in the walls.

Alice shuddered. Was Grandfather's cottage still there at all? Was *Grandfather* still there at all? The thought that he might not be made her walk faster.

There were no wreaths or decorations on any of the ugly buildings, and their presence disoriented her. Was she in the right place at all? She longed for Charlie to appear on the street somewhere and tell her where to go, to be her guiding light as he had been so many times before. Would he remember her the way she remembered him?

Her answer came brutally when she rounded the corner and walked to the place where his cottage was. Or at least, where it used to be. She knew she was right; she recognized the plane tree, though many of its branches had been lopped off. It used to be at the corner of Charlie's cottage where his mother sometimes grew flowers. Now, it sagged in the shadow of an ugly tenement house, three stories high.

Alice stood staring at it for a long, long time, feeling as though a light had gone out in the world. She tried to tell herself that perhaps they had moved, or perhaps they lived in this very tenement building right now. She tried to summon the courage to walk up to the door and knock. But the wind from the sea seemed to be suddenly blowing through her soul, and she could not. Her nerve spent, she turned and struggled onward, toward Grandfather's house.

The relief at the sight of the cottage, unchanged except for the continued weathering of the years, flooded through Alice like a warm tide. There was no wreath or mistletoe here—nor on any of the tenement buildings, she had noticed—but there was a tall figure in the window, with a shock of wild hair spilling over his shoulders.

Tears rolled down Alice's cheeks for the first time that day. She let them roll, feeling them grow cold against her skin, as she strode up to the door. She didn't knock, only pulled it open, and the glad cry sprang from her voice like a released bird.

"Grandpapa."

There was a sharp intake of breath.

"Grandpapa," said Alice, "it's me."

Footsteps shuffled, dragging and slow, and Grandfather appeared in the hallway. His frame was stooped instead of sturdy, his shoulders shrunken. His hair was pure white now and shaggy, his beard thinner than she remembered, but his eyes were still the colour of the sea even if they were reddened and the skin around them sagged. They filled with tears as he held out his arms.

"Allie," he said. "Allie, my poppet."

Alice rushed into his embrace. He held her tightly, with his old, fierce strength, crushed against the warm thudding of his heart. Neither of them moved for a long, long time.

❦

THEY SAT at the kitchen table and made a Christmas dinner of baked potatoes and roast chicken. It was a tiny chicken, more bones than meat, the kind that Grandfather would never have bought even for an ordinary dinner when Alice was still a little girl, but she didn't complain. She would have eaten sawdust and peanut shells if it meant that she could share a meal once more with her grandfather.

As she set the plate down in front of him, Grandfather let out a terrible, wet cough.

"Oh, Grandpapa," said Alice, "are you ill?"

He looked at her with watery eyes and opened his mouth, as if to deny it, then stopped.

"What's the matter?" said Alice. "What does the doctor say?"

"Oh, Allie," Grandfather sighed. "Never mind that right now." He reached over and cupped his hand over hers. "Tell me what happened to you. I went to see Mary last year at Christmas, and you weren't there. She wouldn't tell me where you'd gone." His eyes filled with tears. "I searched for you, but I thought… I thought I had lost you forever."

"Never," said Alice. "No matter how many times you send me away."

Grandfather looked away.

"No, no." Alice leaned forward. "I didn't mean it like that, Grandfather. In fact, I… I finally understand now why you had to do what you did."

He raised his head. "You do?"

Alice told him everything then: about working at the estate, about George Eaton, about Linny and what had happened that very morning. The sorrow in his face deepened with every word she told him.

"You were trying to save me from that, Grandfather," she said. "I'll always be grateful that you did."

"My poppet." Grandfather's eyes shone with pride. "I'm so sorry you went through what you did, but I know now how strong you are."

It had been such a very long time since anyone had been proud of Alice that the words made her eyes fill with tears.

"Tell me about you now," she said. "What's the matter with you?"

"Oh, I don't know."

"But haven't you gotten the doctor?"

"No, poppet, no. There's no money for that," said Grandfather.

Alice stared at him. There had always been money for the doctor when she or one of her sisters was sick.

"The truth is," said Grandfather, "I lost the fish stand in the city, and the one at the docks is ailing. Dorcas oversees it now, but I fear she's stealing me blind. Yet the walk there..." Grandfather hung his head. "I can't always do it anymore."

Alice gripped his hand more tightly.

"Please," she whispered. "This time don't send me away. You're sick, Grandpapa. I can see that. I want to help you. Oh, please, Grandpapa, let me help you."

He studied her for a few long moments before his grip tightened over her hand. "You are not the helpless little girl I sent away," he said. "You have become a woman, my Allie, and I see that you're strong enough to handle whatever London can throw at you."

Alice's shoulders straightened at those words.

"Stay," said Grandfather. "If you will… stay with me."

Alice's tears spilled over. "Forever, Grandpapa."

PART IV

CHAPTER 14

Two Years Later

Alice eyed the scruffy sailor standing in front of the fish stand. Suddenly, the sturdy wooden planks of the counter in front of her didn't feel wide enough.

The man looked her up and down for the third time in thirty seconds, his eyes resting on her chest for a lengthy moment, even though Alice knew that her dark green dress didn't do much to show anything off. She'd made sure of that when she'd bought it. It looked like something a school matron would wear, which was exactly what she had wanted.

"Mister," she said sharply, "are you going to buy some fish or what?"

The man's gaze snapped back to her face, and a sneer twisted his lip. "What kind of tone is that to use when you're speaking to a gentleman?"

Alice held his gaze. "I would certainly never use that tone with a *gentleman*," she said.

Some of the customers in the long queue snickered. Alice flashed them a grin as the man's eyes grew angry.

"Why," he growled, "I should teach you a lesson, you insolent wench."

Alice's fingers closed under the club she kept under the countertop. She pulled it out and rested on the counter, gently, a few inches from his fingers where they rested on the wood. He snatched his hands back. The crowd whooped and laughed.

"That's Alice Thorton, fool." someone shouted. "Don't you know better than to mess with her?"

"Aye, she pried her grandpapa's fish stand from the cold hands of Dorcas Major," said an old woman. "Toughest old biddy on the docks, but Alice is tougher."

The man recoiled, still staring at the club.

"What's it going to be, chum?" Alice demanded. "Do you want some fish or not?"

The man turned and hurried off. Alice shook her head, sliding the club back underneath the counter, then turned to her next customer. "Sorry about that, Mrs. Tillman."

Time had been unkind to Charlie's mother. Meg's hair was a collection of grey strings hanging hopelessly around her head, and her smile was nearly lost in the mass of wrinkles that her face had become.

"It's quite all right, Alice," she said. "I know it's not easy being a woman alone in these parts."

She knew it all too well; Brock had died three years ago, before Alice's return to the docks.

"That's true," said Alice. "One cod?"

"That's right."

Alice prepared the fish, wrapping it in newspaper. "Any..." She paused. "Any word from Charlie?"

Meg looked away. "I'm sorry, dear. None."

Charlie had gone out to sea the spring before Alice came home, right after his father died. The voyage was a long one of exploration. No one really knew when the ship would be back.

That was what Meg said all the time, anyway. Alice's heart told her that three years was longer than any ship would be gone.

She handed the fish over the counter. "Here you are, Mrs. Tillman."

"Thank you, dear," said Meg. "How is your grandfather?"

Alice's smile faltered even more. "Ailing," she admitted. "But I'm there for him."

"It must be hard on you, dear, running the business and looking after him." Meg took the fish. "He's lucky to have you."

She hurried off, and Alice stared after her, gripping a ball of newspaper wadded tight in her hands. Thinking of Charlie.

***

"Grandpapa." Alice shut the front door behind her and hung her coat on a peg. "I'm home."

The feeble response came from the living room. They had moved Grandfather out of his bedroom when it had become clear that the walk down the hallway was too much for him. He lay now where he did all day, every day, on the narrow bed in the corner of the living room, swaddled head to foot in blankets against the wintry chill.

Today was a good day, Alice saw. He'd had the strength to add some wood to the fire, and it crackled merrily in the hearth. But the effort had taken all of the strength out of him; he lay on the cot with lips pursed, every breath crackling, a blue line around his mouth.

"Hello, Grandpapa." Alice knelt beside him.

"Allie... my poppet," he wheezed. His hand twitched weakly, and she wrapped it in hers. Pride and love shone in his eyes, and he reached up to caress her cheek.

"How do you feel?" she asked.

"Fine, poppet, fine," he said as he always did.

She knew he didn't, but also knew that there was nothing she could do; nor could the doctors. They said that it was his heart, and there was nothing to be done. If she thought about it for too long, she would scream, so she did not. She only said, "Would you like some tea?"

He nodded weakly, and she brewed two identical cups, just the way they liked them. She sat on the edge of Grandfather's bed while they both drank and gazed out of the window at the lights of fishing-boats on the sea, slowly coming into the docks.

"Cold out tonight," said Alice. She put a little more wood on the fire. Though she hadn't been able to reclaim the fishing stand in the city, at least their days of worrying over food and fuel were over.

"Very... cold," Grandfather wheezed. "Almost... Christmas."

Alice looked up at him. "Almost Christmas. Why, Grandfather, you're right." It was only two weeks away; Alice had barely noticed as the months blended and became December once more.

He smiled, his eyes bright, and Alice was flooded with the warm memories of last Christmas. It had been a year to the day since she'd left the estate, and there had been enough money for a roast goose, even if it was trimmed with potatoes and onions instead of the sumptuous stuffings she'd seen at Eaton, and even if they had shared it with all their new neighbours instead of a plethora of well-off family. Grandfather had still been well enough to walk around the house then, and he'd sat at the head of the table, laughing his great booming laugh.

Now that laugh was a sad echo of its former self, but the light in his eyes was still there. "I... love... Christmas," he said. "Now that... you're here."

"Oh, Grandpapa." Alice wrapped her hand around his. "So do I." She prayed that he would live long enough to see just one more before he could rest at last.

"Wish...," said Grandfather, then coughed and wheezed. Alice rubbed his back.

"Wish... your sisters... could... be... here," he finally finished.

"It's as you said," said Alice. "We protected them well enough that they wouldn't know how to survive out here. They're all right, Grandpapa, I know they are."

That last part was not entirely true, but Alice did not allow herself to think about it until late that night when Grandfather had eaten a small supper and fallen asleep on the cot.

It was only then that she went up to the room she'd once shared with her two sisters, a room that still felt large and cold and empty without them. The tiny desk in the corner held the notebook she'd bought when she still worked with the estate, its pages now thick with her messy writing, as well as a few new sheets of paper and a longer bit of pencil, and an envelope.

Alice took out the contents of the envelope and read, slowly and painstakingly, although not quite as slowly as she had penned the words.

Dere Bettie *and Hestur*

I miss you. I hop you are wel. Is Mary treeting you wel? I saw you reeding last Crismus. I hop you can reed this.

I nevur stoped loving you. Granpapa is sik. Pleze rite bak.

Love,

Alis.

. . .

A TEAR DRIPPED onto the page; it was marked with spots and wrinkles from former tears that had done the same. Alice drew the back of her hand over her face to wipe them away. Then she folded up the page and returned it to the envelope, glimpsing the red words stamped on the back as she slipped it into its drawer.

RETURN TO SENDER.

IN THE FACE of the many changes that had taken place in the neighbourhood, somehow the little church where Alice had been baptized and her parents buried still stood. Despite the bitter cold that Christmas Eve, Alice pushed the window in the living room open, allowing in a frigid draft as well as the distant sound of Christmas carols being sung in that same church.

"Listen, Grandpapa." she said.

It was almost a surprise when her grandfather opened his eyes. They were rheumy and vague, distant. The doctor had given him some medicine that smelled strong and made him sleepy. Alice was grateful—it had eased the deep lines of suffering around her grandfather's mouth and eyes—but it still made him seem like he was very far away at times.

"Hmmm?" he croaked.

"Listen," said Alice. She left the open window and sat beside him, tucking a rug around his shoulders to shield him from the draft.

"What?" said Grandpapa.

Alice held a finger to her lips and sat on the bed beside him. They both were silent for a few long moments, and the notes of the organ made its way into the house alongside the soft sounds of the singing congregation.

God rest ye merry, gentlemen,

Let nothing you dismay.

Grandfather's lips twitched upward. Narrow though the bed was, there was just enough room for Alice to lie down beside him and press her skinny frame against her grandfather's skeletal body. He draped an arm over her shoulders, and they lay side by side. His breath rattled and whistled in her ear, but when she rested her head against his chest, the thump of his heart seemed as steady as ever.

Remember Christ our Saviour

was born on Christmas Day.

Alice closed her eyes and allowed the carol to wash over her, heedless of the cold wind on her skin. She listened to Grandfather's softly thumping heart as it grew slower. She allowed the words to sink deep into her, reminding her that whether or not she hated Christmas, whether or not it held gifts or decorated trees or roast goose dinners, it was still a thing of glory. A thing of hope. A thing of salvation.

To save us all from Satan's pow'r

when we were gone astray.

Grandfather's hand tangled in her hair, stroking her back gently. A tear rolled down Alice's cheek. His breaths were very slow now, wet and difficult, and his heart had slowed to a soft, dull flutter. Yet Alice could not shake the thought that he was safer now than he had ever been. He was on his way home.

"I love you, Grandpapa," she whispered.

"Alice... I love... you, my poppet," Grandfather murmured.

Oh, tidings of comfort and joy

Comfort and joy

Oh, tidings of comfort and joy.

Grandfather's heart grew slower and slower. Alice kept her eyes closed, knowing there was nothing in the world that she could or should do other than to be here with him.

Before the carol came to an end, the thuds of Grandfather's heart grew quieter and quieter until Alice could no longer hear them. A last breath brushed against the back of her neck. Then he was still.

Alice squeezed her eyes tightly shut. The tears rolled down her cheeks, faster and faster. They were filled with utter mourning, yes. A sorrow that penetrated deep into the pit of her soul; an agony far deeper than she had ever known the human heart could possibly endure.

Yet in that mourning, comfort and joy still lived, for Alice knew that Grandfather had gone quietly into the loving arms of the One whose hope filled Christmases of every kind, even this one.

CHAPTER 15

IT WAS ONLY because the vicar had been friends with Grandfather since they were boys that Alice could have him buried on the very next day.

The Christmas Day service was over, and the congregation—shrunken now in the face of the growing tenements full of scoundrels—had all gone home to what meagre lunches and half-happy families they had. As for Grandfather, there was no real funeral. Apart from Alice and Meg and the vicar, no one was left who loved him. She had thought of trying to write to Mary, but she knew Grandfather had tried that many, many times, and the letters always came back unopened.

So it was that it was only Alice and the vicar and Meg in the cemetery that afternoon, and the vicar did not stay long; he had another service that evening. He only said the necessary words and stayed long enough for the gravediggers to shovel the last of the dirt over Grandfather's grave. The headstone was small and blank—Alice had not been able to find anyone who would carve it on Christmas Day. But it lay between the headstones of her mother and her grandmother, right where Grandfather had wanted. There would be no pauper's grave for him.

Meg squeezed Alice's arm. "I'm sorry, dear."

Alice took deep breaths, trying to hold back the hard knot of tears that threatened to spill over. In the brutal daylight, staring down at the fresh, cold earth where her grandfather's body now lay, the hope that had suffused her last night seemed a very, very long way away. All she could think of now was how the dear hands that had held hers, and the dear mouth that had smiled at her, and the dear old heart that had beaten so faithfully with love to the very end now lay there beneath the soil. *He must be so cold,* she thought. She was gripped with an irrational urge to tear that dirt aside, pull his motionless body from the coffin and wrap him in rugs and blankets like she'd done every morning before going out to the fish stand.

"I'm so glad you came back," said Meg softly. "He was loved to the very end, and he knew it. I used to stop by him now and then in the daytime if you were still away, and there was only one thing he ever talked about." She smiled through her tears. "How much he loved you, and how proud of you he was."

Alice laid her hand over Meg's. "Thank you, Mrs. Tillman."

"I wish I could help you, dear. I wish I was anything except barely surviving myself." Meg struggled with her tears. "But if you think of anything..."

"I'll be fine," said Alice.

Meg's mouth twitched with sorrow, and she could say nothing. She only nodded, patted Alice's arm a last time, and then turned to hurry away, weeping.

Alice bowed her head. It had just begun to snow. The shining flakes, as yet unsullied by putrid London, landed like tiny stars on the smooth grey of Grandfather's headstone.

"Oh, Grandpapa," she whispered. "Whatever am I to do without you?"

She received no response but the howl of the wind. There would be no more caring for Grandfather, no more hoping for Grandfather, no more laughing with Grandfather. He was gone, and the reality felt as heavy as though her heart had been replaced with a tombstone.

There was nothing more for Alice here; she was suddenly and desperately reminded that he wasn't here. A great emptiness yawned before her, containing only a shell. He was gone.

Alice hurried to Grandfather's—to *her*—cottage with tears rolling helplessly down her cheeks. Only to sit there in the abundant silence, wondering what to do with herself.

The *Bold Lady* cut through the wintry waves with fierce aggression despite her significant port-ward list, and the tattered condition of her sails. Her name was no longer visible on her gunwale; it had been torn apart by the same storm off the coast of Africa that had nearly drowned them all, the storm that had run the *Bold Lady* aground on the rocky coastline of some nation that had never seen Europeans before, yet had been nonetheless kind and generous with food, fire and shelter while the *Bold Lady's* crew tried to figure out how they would ever get home.

Even after they had done their best to repair their ship, the crew had known as they set off that their chances of ever seeing land again were limited, let alone making it back to England. Yet here they were, plunging through this midwinter's day, riding the grey waves that tossed the hapless *Bold Lady* back and forth, and the ship carried on as bravely as her namesake.

High on the crow's nest, Charlie Tillman had grown used to the buck and tip of the ship underneath him. The tilting floor couldn't shake him loose; he steadied himself with just a hand on the mast as he squinted against the grey gloom of the day, his heart thundering with hope.

It had only been when they landed in Cornwall a few days ago that the crew had realized it was nearly Christmas. Days, weeks, and months had blended into one another as the tropical seasons failed to mark the passing of time when they were marooned in the wilderness. When they reached Cornwall at last, they had seen the wreaths on the doorways, and the captain had said, "Boys, what if we were home for Christmas?"

So it was that the last mad part of the voyage began, the struggling haul up the English Channel in the middle of winter in a crazy effort to be home for Christmas. Today, Charlie knew, was Christmas Day, and it was wearing on into the afternoon. If they wrecked now, this would all have been for nothing.

If they did not, he would be able to feel his mother's arms around him for the first time in three years.

He wondered if Ma was still in London at all. As he often did, he feared that losing Charlie on top of losing Pa would have been too much for her. But he pushed the thought aside. Ma was the toughest person he knew... apart from Alice Thorton.

Feeling the cold kiss of snow on his face, Charlie closed his eyes, warmed from the inside by his memories of Alice. The softness in her eyes, the strength around the set of her mouth, the black curly torrent of her hair that never quite played along with her. It had been so long since he had last seen her. She had been twelve then; she would be seventeen now, and he could only imagine that she had grown even more beautiful.

He opened his eyes and shook himself. It was a foolish thing, really, to be so smitten with a girl he'd last seen when they were children. Perhaps she had moved on by now. Seventeen... maybe she was being courted by someone out there in Edgeword, a nice farm hand, or maybe even a farmer. Perhaps she had a whole life of safety planned out for her. Could he blame her if she'd given her heart to another? He could only imagine that she—that everyone—had assumed that he was as lost as the rest of the *Bold Lady's* crew must have been presumed to be.

No, Charlie decided. He would not blame her, but he would mourn, for though it had been so long since they had been together, Charlie knew that he had only ever loved one girl, and it was Alice.

He squinted against the swirling wind and grey fog. Had he spotted something—a flicker of light, the outline of land? His imagination, maybe, or his eyes were scrambled from so much time spent squinting at a bare horizon, longing for the sight of a ship full of rescuers or enemies or anyone who could bring him back home... But no. There it was again. A flash of light. An outline of buildings on the horizon.

Charlie laughed. Mad though they were, they had made it home for Christmas after all. He breathed in deeply and gave full throat to his cry, making sure it would be heard throughout the ship.

"Land ho."

I SAW three ships come sailing in on Christmas day, on Christmas day

I saw three ships come sailing in on Christmas day in the morning.

Alice shut the kitchen window, cutting off the sound of the three little boys next door—not as little as they once were, but still young enough to run around the garden of the new tenement building with their toy ships—as they played and sang. She drew the curtains shut and went toward the living room, but the sight of Grandfather's bed, rumpled and unmade, was too much for her.

She tried the kitchen next. Had she eaten yet today? She didn't think so. Meg had said something about bringing her some bread that evening. Alice hoped she wouldn't. She'd already ruined enough of poor Meg's Christmas, and heaven knew that Meg didn't have much of a Christmas to start with, alone in her tiny tenement with her ever-sickly daughter.

No, it was time for the rest of the world to enjoy their Christmas, no matter how forlorn or lonely Alice's had turned out to be.

There was food in the cupboards, but Alice couldn't summon the wherewithal to compose so much as a sandwich or cut a piece of cheese. She touched the kettle, thought of how she would never make tea for two again, and left.

In the end she settled in her bedroom, curled on her side on her unmade bed, and stared at the wall waiting for sleep to come even though she was still fully dressed, and the sun still shone outside. She tried not to think of Grandfather or Betty or Hester or Linny or dear, sweet Charlie and how she would never see any of them ever again.

Above all, she tried not to think of what she would *do* now. Her life had become a steady stream of running the fish stand and caring for Grandfather. Now... what? Run the fish stand, come home and sit here in the silence with no one?

She squeezed her eyes tightly shut, but the tears escaped anywhere, shaking her body as they flowed from her in broken sobs. The hope she'd felt last night had ebbed because it had belonged to Grandfather. As always, the glory of Christmas was something that had never belonged to her. It was for someone else; she was an observer on the outside, the scullery-maid who washed the dishes after the feast, the girl left behind while her grandfather went on to enjoy in full the implications of the Christmas miracle.

When she heard the knock, it was loud and insistent, like someone had been out there knocking for a long time. Alice groaned and pulled her blankets over her head. She didn't want to talk to Meg and see the pity in her eyes. She only wanted peace and silence.

The knock came again, louder, and Alice felt a pang of guilt. Meg was only trying to help. She pushed back the covers and hauled herself to her feet, so exhausted that her head felt as though it was floating somewhere above her body instead of actually being attached to her as she dragged her sore feet down the hallway to the door.

"Hello?" she called softly, with the wariness that Grandfather had taught her.

There was a long silence. Then the voice came. "*Alice?*"

Alice froze. She must be hallucinating, she thought. The exhaustion and grief were all too much for her. It was impossible that the voice could be the one she thought she had heard, deep and warm, filled with wonder.

It was impossible that Charlie was standing outside this door. It simply could not be. Nothing that wonderful ever happened to Alice.

The voice came again. "Allie, are you in there?"

Alice's breath caught. She reached out very slowly, with a hand that trembled uncontrollably, and grasped the doorknob, but she couldn't turn it. If she opened that door and saw nothing but the cold, empty street, she thought she would die right where she stood.

"Alice?" Charlie called again.

Whether or not he was a ghost or a dream, it didn't matter. She had to look into his eyes one more time. Summoning her courage, Alice flung the door wide open, and there he was.

Hopelessly tattered, his clothes hanging from his frame in rags, the skin goose-pimpled where the wind blew through on his knees and elbows, a blanket clutched around his shoulders for warmth. His hair was long and wild, tossing in the wind in a torrential black mane. His skin was copper-dark and lined with sun. But his were eyes as blue as they ever were, pure as they ever were. He was her Charlie, alive and in the flesh. She could never have imagined him like this, not with his shoulders so broad or his skin so brown.

"Charlie?" she whispered.

He didn't move; he was too busy staring at her, the way a lost man would stare at the north star that would guide him finally home after a storm.

Alice's heart hammered. He was here, but why? Could her wild hope be true? Surely not. If he was alive, if he had stayed away so long, then surely, he no longer cared for her.

"Oh, Alice," he said. "I thought I'd never see you again."

Alice fought back her tears, clinging to her toughness like a shield. "What are you doing here?"

He laughed, the sound she loved so well. "Where else would I go?" he said. "For three years, all I've thought about is coming home to find you."

Wild hope leaped in her.

Charlie shivered. "May I come in?"

"OSh—yes. Yes. Of course. You're freezing. Tea?" said Alice.

She shut the door behind him and let him into the kitchen, and it seemed so much less empty when he sat at the table. She put the teapot on the stove with shaking hands.

"Ma told me about Mr. Pryor," said Charlie. "I'm sorry."

"So am I," said Alice. "I miss him already." She swallowed her tears again.

"I'm sorry that I wasn't here to help," said Charlie. He stared down at the table. "I'm sorry that I wasn't here for any of it."

Alice set his mug of tea in front of him and sat down opposite him. Charlie grasped the mug and sucked down gulps of tea like he hadn't seen any in months. He set the mug down and winced. "Sorry. That was a little rude."

"You, ah, must have been thirsty," said Alice.

"I was," Charlie admitted. He brushed the back of his hand over his mouth. "I hear on the docks that you have quite a reputation. Alice Thorton, the toughest woman in London." His eyes shone. "I'm glad others finally see the fire in you."

Alice couldn't help smiling.

"When did you come back to London?" Charlie asked.

Alice couldn't stop herself. She told him everything then, leaving out none of the details. His eyes darkened to stormy blue when she told him about George Eaton, and his hands clenched into white-knuckled fists on the table. But as she told him about rooting Dorcas out of the fish stand and getting her grandfather's business back on its feet, his eyes softened into love and pride.

"You have done incredible things, Allie," he said. "I wish I'd been here to see them."

"Where *were* you, Charlie?" she asked softly.

He told her a story that she could hardly have believed if he wasn't the living evidence of it, sitting right here across the table from her, about a shipwreck off the coast of Africa and a three-year struggle to survive and rebuild the ship. And then a last, valiant voyage, fighting against the odds, to get home for Christmas.

"We made it," he said. "I can't believe we made it."

Alice no longer heeded the tears that rolled down her cheeks. "Oh, Charlie, how did you do it?" she cried. "How did you find the courage and the resilience to keep going through all of that?"

Charlie reached his hands over the table. Hesitantly, Alice allowed him to take hers.

"There was only one reason," he said, "and it was you. It was always you."

Alice's body shivered with hope and terror.

Then he spoke the words she'd been longing for since she could remember.

"I love you, Alice," he said, "and I want to marry you. Please... may I?"

She thought it must be strange that a man she hadn't seen in five years would propose so quickly, but it didn't feel strange at all. It felt like the most natural thing in the world. And her answer came just as naturally, the way morning comes after darkness.

"Yes," she cried. "Oh, Charlie, yes."

She was out of her chair then and in his arms, and he held her in the warm kitchen while the boys outside sang Christmas hymns and the world had never been more beautiful than at that moment.

"There's—there's only one thing." Alice stepped back, brushing away her happy tears.

"What is it, my love?" asked Charlie. "Whatever it is, I'll do whatever it takes to make it better."

"I don't know that you can," said Alice, smiling into his loving eyes. "I don't know where you'll be able to find work in London. Surely... surely, you'll have to go out to sea, I suppose?"

Charlie laughed. "That's right. I never told you. Allie, neither of us have to worry about any of that. I've got enough money to start any kind of business that I want."

Alice stared at his ragged clothes.

"We found a great chest of buried Portuguese gold on that same coastline," said Charlie. "The native people told us that a pirate ship had sunk near there; the pirates never made it home, but they left their gold. The people had no use for it. They told us to take it with us. We shared it between the whole crew, and, well—"

"Oh, Charlie," Alice laughed and hugged him tightly. "Do the miracles never end?"

Charlie held her close.

"No," he said. "Thanks to Christmas, the miracles never do."

EPILOGUE

CHAPTER 1

One Year Later

The village had changed so little in three years that Alice felt as though she had walked backwards in time. She kept her cloak wrapped tightly around her shoulders as her feet crunched in the snow of the square. The tree at its centre was splendidly decorated, all hung with ribbons and candy canes, but no one was outside now. Snow blew against her face on the wind, dusting the wreaths and mistletoe on every house.

She brushed some of the snowflakes from her eyelashes and squared her shoulders as she approached the farmhouse. Warm golden light pooled on the snowy ground outside, but Alice forced herself not to look through that window into that hateful drawing room. Instead, she knocked twice on the door, then stepped back and waited.

There was a burst of laughter from inside. Alice squared her shoulders.

The door swung open, and Alice's jaw dropped. "Hester?" she whispered.

The girl standing in the doorway was tall and slender, her body just beginning to swell with the curves of womanhood. She gazed at Alice with limpid dark eyes. Her hair was held back by a bright blue ribbon, and she held a book in one hand, her index finger tucked between the pages to mark her place.

Her eyes widened. "Alice, is that you?"

"Oh, Hester, look at you." cried Alice. "You've gotten so tall."

Hester smiled and stepped forward, then hesitated, a shadow crossing over her face. "You... you're wearing a nice dress."

Alice glanced down. The dress was emerald green, like the last one, but this one modestly celebrated her curves and hugged her figure. She had no need to fear when she walked the streets of London anymore, not when her husband and his legendary status accompanied her.

"Thank you," she said.

"But I thought—" Hester blinked. "Mary said—"

"Hester." Betty's strident voice called from within. "Who are you talking to?"

The years had done nothing to change the pinched, sharp quality of Betty's features. She'd grown beautiful, in an icy way, and she seemed as rosy-cheeked and bright-eyed as Hester as she walked up beside her sister and put a protective arm around her shoulders.

"Betty, look." said Hester. "It's Alice, and she's—she's not what Mama Mary said she was, is she? They—they don't dress like that."

Betty's eyes burned into Alice's with acidic hatred for a long, fierce moment.

"Don't let appearances deceive you, Hester," she said bitterly. "Alice got us into this mess in the first place, and she's just the same as she always was. Selfish."

"Betty, I can explain." Alice stepped forward. "Please, listen to me, and you'll see that maybe the truth isn't what you've been taught."

"Why are you here?" Betty demanded. "What do you want?"

"Just to know my sisters," said Alice. "And to help you, if there's anything I can do for you."

"Oh," said Hester, "you could—"

"I think it's time you left," said Betty.

"But Betty—" Hester began.

Betty pulled her closer. "Don't come back, Alice. We don't want you."

The words trampled upon the old wound in Alice's heart that she thought might never heal.

"I'll never stop loving you," she said softly. "If you ever need anything, come to find me."

"We don't," said Betty. "Nothing from *you*."

Hester's eyes were filled with tears. "Goodbye, Alice."

"Goodbye," said Alice, and the door slammed shut in her face.

***

Everything in Alice's world was cold, except for the warmth of Charlie's hand in her own.

The grey sea tossed furiously against the windblown beach, the waves wild and vengeful, capped with dirty white. Spots of black flotsam dotted the ocean, and the horizon was blurred by fog. The beach itself was empty except for Alice, Charlie, and the heaps of driftwood washed to shore by last night's storm.

"How about this one?" Charlie asked. He paused and pointed at a gnarled log lying half-buried in the sand.

Alice shook her head. "No, no. It doesn't have branches."

Charlie laughed as they kept walking. "You're quite right. Where would we hang the decorations?"

Alice grinned up at him, the smile coming so easily. He returned it. It was so easy to lose herself in his soft blue eyes and to forget the shadows of her past that sometimes seemed ready to drag her down. One smile from Charlie banished them all.

"I'm sorry it didn't go well in Edgeword yesterday," said Charlie.

Alice squeezed his hand. "I didn't think that it would, but I was still sorry."

"Of course, you were. Your sisters meant everything to you." Charlie sighed.

"They're safe," Alice shrugged. "It hurts, but I know I don't need them." She leaned against him. "I have all the family that I need right here."

"And right *here*," said Charlie, brushing his fingertips against her midriff.

The swelling of her belly was barely visible, but Alice smiled. "That's right."

"And we're going to find a driftwood Christmas tree this year," Charlie added stubbornly. "Just like your favorite one that you ever had."

"Otherwise, we'll go and get one," said Alice. "We can."

They could do almost anything they liked, she felt. Charlie's investment had turned the fish stand into a proper fishmonger's shop, and it made her feel as though anything was possible, especially after they'd bought the piece of land next to the cottage. It had contained a run-down house destined to become another ugly tenement, but they'd knocked it down and converted it into a park. Their child, Alice thought, would play there. Their baby would never feel trapped or scared or alone like she had.

"We're getting a driftwood one," said Charlie firmly, "like the one you wanted."

Alice smiled. Immediately, she could tell that there were no magical driftwood trees on the beach. It would have been nice if this could be the year that echoed that Christmas miracle that had lit up her world with Grandfather and her sisters that one year, but the world didn't work that way. Things didn't always work out perfectly.

Charlie pointed. "Look. Right over there."

He let go of her hand and raced off across the sand, and Alice stood and watched him go, his hair blowing in the wind, his laugh filling his world.

No, things didn't always work out perfectly on this side of heaven. But sometimes... just sometimes... they did.

The End

CONTINUE READING...

Thank you for reading **Grandfather's Christmas Orphans!** Why not read **The Cotton Mill Orphan**? **Here's a sneak peek for you:**

Juliette Purcell couldn't stop thinking of the piece of bread in the wooden crate.

She sat cross-legged on the sleeping pallet, trying her best to focus on gazing out of the window, or rather, out of the single windowpane that still had any glass in it. The big square window once had four panes. Now only one remained, small and grimy; the other three were boarded up, with cardboard stuffed into the cracks between the bits of rotten wood and the rusted edges of the window frame.

Still, it offered more than most of the little tenements inside this building had: a view of the outside world. Sleet drummed

THANKS FOR READING

If you love Victorian Romance, **Click Here**

https://victorian.subscribemenow.com/

to hear about all **New Faye Godwin Romance Releases! I will let you know as soon as they become available!**

Thank you, Friends! If you enjoyed ***Grandfather's Christmas Orphans,*** would you kindly take a couple minutes to leave a positive review on Amazon? It only takes a moment, and positive reviews truly make a difference. Thank you so much! I appreciate it!

Much love,

Faye Godwin

MORE FAYE GODWIN VICTORIAN ROMANCES!

We love rich, dramatic Victorian Romances and have a library of Faye Godwin titles just for you! (Remember that ALL of Faye's Victorian titles can be downloaded FREE with Kindle Unlimited!)

CLICK HERE to discover Faye's Complete Collection of Victorian Romance!

https://ticahousepublishing.com/victorian-romance.html

ABOUT THE AUTHOR

Faye Godwin has been fascinated with Victorian Romance since she was a teen. After reading every Victorian Romance in her public library, she decided to start writing them herself —which she's been doing ever since. Faye lives with her husband and young son in England. She loves to travel throughout her country, dreaming up new plots for her romances. She's delighted to join the Tica House Publishing family and looks forward to getting to know her readers.

contact@ticahousepublishing.com